# Animals

By J. E. Lynch

For Carla, with love

*"Do wolves make myths of men? Do they create stories in which humans are seen as examples of the ultimate embodiment of good or evil? They do not. To the wolf a human being is just another animal."- Large Mammals of North America by L. F. Menslip*

*"If I wanted a one-sentence definition of human beings, this would do: humans are the animals that believe the stories they tell about themselves...each story has what we might call a dark side; it casts a shadow." The Philosopher and the Wolf by Mark Rowlands.*

The story that follows concerns the shadows of the stories we tell about ourselves and other animals.

In the beginning… I often walk at night. There's no need to explain all the reasons why just now. More importantly, I walk in darkness. Darkness and night do not always go together in our world of electric lights and twenty-four hour living but when you put them together they have a special effect on the mind.

Walk at night in near total darkness and your senses are stimulated; you hear all the sounds of calling and moving animals. You see glimpses of movement that you can't quite grasp, your brain works furiously to make sense of it all and it is TERRIFYING.

Fascinating but terrifying.

Walking alone at night in lonely places is a time machine. It will take you back into the past. It will take you ten thousand years back into the past in an instant.

In a single hour you will find that you are creating a mythology in your mind. You will be imagining dreadful spirits, ghosts, ghouls, werewolves, other strange and hideous beasts and fearful animal-headed gods in the darkness. This mythology will be your own but also it will borrow from stories and parts of stories you have read and heard, whole or in part, remembered with perfect clarity or buried deep in the caves, caverns and other dark places of your memory. It will be your personal picture of the universe, visible and invisible but will also connect you to people who lived long ages ago and left the marks of their dreams and nightmares in the land you now call your own.

You will, and this effect is heightened if it's a cold night, imagine yourself building a camp fire and that camp fire being civilisation, the whole of civilisation and all beyond its light being alien and well…
TERRIFYING.

The whole of the natural and supernatural worlds are beyond that circle of light in your mind now and they have their own motivations and desires and you may be no more than a meal for some of the things that populate those worlds.

Then you think some more and wonder if there might be worse things you could end up being than a meal.

And then, naturally, you think 'what if'; what if all those figures out there in the darkness, or in your mind, or in the darkness of your mind, that have been waiting back there in the deepest, darkest corner of your mind, were real?

...and perhaps you still have quite a long way to go before you reach home.

# Part One- Shadows on the cave wall

Chapter 1

Chiang Mai is a small city in the north of Thailand. It's not far from the border with China. Around it there is a great deal of beautiful countryside. There are forests of large trees of a deep green that has taken thousands of years of rain, growth, decay and regrowth to produce. There are waterfalls and farmland and a feeling of a world that is old and new; constant and always changing, all at the same time.

Like many cities Chiang Mai is always being built at the edges. Men and women with skin tanned to the colour of the darkest and oldest trees in the forests work hard for long hours at building layers of concrete one on top of the other. When the buildings are finished they are absorbed into the city, becoming like a ring in the trunk of a great tree, a new layer is started with new buildings and so it goes on.

Take a deep breath please. Close your eyes. Imagine you are an animal, a dog perhaps, running through the streets of the city from its outer suburbs inwards, focusing on nothing and everything at the same time, moving fast, with a purpose. You get to the centre of the city through apartment buildings, schools, shops, garages, offices, and in the end, more and more restaurants and bars. The centre of the city is where you find the tourists and the things that tourists are drawn to and that the presence of tourists creates.

It's busy there at almost every hour of the day or night with people from many countries. Pale or sunburnt Europeans move about between the restaurants and bars that line both banks of the river, dirty and dark, that runs through downtown. Australian and American accents compete for space in air that is already nearly full with the smells of food cooking in the small kitchens and on the street food stalls.

Now bring yourself back to your human body and let go of the heightened senses of the dog.

It's noisy and crowded and you need to watch your back and your pocket in certain parts, just like in any city.

Now that you have seen the city, notice a new arrival.

A girl of thirteen years old or thereabouts.

A European child alone in Chiang Mai should have drawn attention but she moved with such physical assurance that she drew none. It was as if she moved faster than the city's attention could follow. She was neither big nor small for her age but she moved like an athlete. She seemed to know where she was going but not because she had been there before, more by instinct.

There was an unusual quality to the way she moved. It would have been very hard to explain even if you had taken the time to study her movement. The fact was it was all about how she used her senses. She navigated as much by sound and smell as by sight which made her look not altogether human. Her movement was graceful but you would not have been wrong if you compared it to the movement of a rat.

(Rats, of course, don't get the respect they deserve, as no one moves more efficiently in a city than a rat.)

The city stank of cigarettes everywhere, even when no smoker was to be seen. They had scent marked the streets. There was also the smell of sewage mixed with that of freshly squeezed orange juice and barbecued sweet corn. The sweet smell of the fruit distracted the girl's attention for a moment, but only a moment. She travelled unerringly towards her destination.

Down a narrow back street there was a small garage. No work seemed to be going on there on this particular day. From the street you could see two men inside. Both were large men, powerful although they had big bellies. They looked like what they were, ex soldiers starting to fall out of shape. The falling had begun around their middles.

In the back there was a small office and in it was another man at a computer. He was a tall, sharp-faced man; hard and capable looking. He was wearing the latest home strip Manchester United football jersey. There was not a single speck of oil or grease on that jersey.

The girl entered the garage without hesitation. She moved remarkably quickly. The first of the two men was dead before he was aware of any threat, as she had hoped. That was usually the way. The hard work started with the second man.

Any way you react in a situation of violence will leave a weakness somewhere; in your posture, your guard, your balance, your timing. The girl knew this very well. She moved fluidly under the straight right punch that he threw, tackled him to the ground and broke his neck.

A little too slow.

The man from the office was out in the garage now and ready to fight. Still, he was on his own and the girl was less hurried. The man took a boxing stance and she noticed the blade of a sharp knife protruding from the bottom of his left fist. So he would use the knife but he was not 'knife crazy', she could not simply concentrate on attacks with the blade. He would use the knife to disguise and set-up punches; punches to set up the use of the blade. He knew what he was doing.

She moved quickly, avoiding strikes and kicked one of his knees. As he rebalanced she grasped his left wrist with both of her hands and drove her head upwards into his jaw. Seconds later he was dead by his own knife.

The girl checked herself over for damage. She was not surprised to find that she was cut on her own left arm, above the wrist. There was no immediate danger and the pain would not begin until the adrenalin started to leave her body.

She looked about her for any surveillance cameras that might be present but there were none.

She walked to the back of the office and opened the door to a storage room at the back. When she switched on the light she could see that the room was full of cages. In each small cage there was an animal. Maybe thirty of them, wild creatures- exhausted, scared, tired. She looked into the eyes of chivet cats and small monkeys destined to be sold as pets. The cages were dirty. The smell was dreadful. For the first time that day the girl hesitated. Then one by one and crying softly all the time, she removed the animals from their cages and killed them as swiftly and gently as she was able.

Chapter 2

Afterwards there was no time to waste. Making distance was critical now. Outside the garage she had noticed several small motorcycles and she found the keys to one of them quickly.

The girl had ridden motorcycles before. She would have found it difficult to admit even to herself, since she had been trained to view machines with a certain suspicion; taught to rely on her own resources first and foremost, but she loved to travel on two wheels.

This bike was a Chinese model 175cc with a red tank and five gears. It had a small engine but it was light and fairly fast. The balance and movement needed to ride well felt natural and enjoyable to her. She was still tense in mind and body after killing the captive animals. As she pulled away from the garage and the carnage she was leaving behind her there; the sensations, the balance and movement of riding the motorcycle, began to relax her. She moved up through the gears and took in a deep breath. Her mind cleared and she purged herself of the fear, anger and horror of her work.

She filled the petrol tank on her way out of the city, paying with some money she had taken from the pocket of the man with the football shirt. She took money when she needed it and spent it as she needed to; she had no feeling that money belonged to anyone in particular. Just the same with the motorbike, she used things as she found them and left them when she had no more immediate use for them. She had no real notion of ownership and no sense of attachment to things.

She travelled north at first. She left Chiang Mai and its busy traffic, in which she was just another motorcyclist among many, behind and was soon in the countryside and almost alone on the road. It had rained and the tarmac was a little wet. She opened the throttle fully and felt nothing but the speed.

She passed through villages as the roads brought her uphill. A pattern emerged as she passed village, farmland, dense forest, farmland then village again; the constant interplay between the human and the natural worlds. She almost stopped at a wooden stall by the side of the road where a man with a home-made single-shot rifle was selling squirrels he had hunted and hung with string from a thin wooden stick; but that was not part of the mission so the man got a pass that day.

Her course turned north east as the hills became steeper and she stopped for the night and hid the motorbike among some trees. She passed into the forest and washed in a small waterfall. She made a fire and ate some nuts and dried mushrooms she carried with her. The mushrooms; which where Chinese and known as Chaga, had the special property of increasing her physical endurance and they were a staple of her provisions when on a mission.

As she ate she felt a movement near her in the undergrowth. Then she heard the sound, a gentle rustling. She fixed her eyes on a spot about five feet away as a large grey snake rose to face her. It was tall when it raised itself up like this, nearly as tall as she was. They looked at each other for a few moments. She didn't smile as many animals find a smile aggressive because it involves showing teeth. She showed the snake the food she was eating and it had no interest in it. It lowered itself slowly, with some dignity and then moved slowly away.

The girl continued eating slowly. She had quite a long way yet to travel and the provisions she had with her would see her return to her destination severely hungry at best. She was used however to living on little and making it last.

The sky was as bright as it was dark, countless stars illuminating a background of the most vibrant black. There were more noises in the night and eyes shining in the blackness but she closed her eyes as if she were alone and slowly leaned back until she was lying on the ground. The ground was soft, covered as it was in a thick blanket of fallen and decaying leaves.

On nights like this when she had finished a job and she was alone under such a sky she felt more free than at any other time. Her work was done and she was yet to be given a new mission. The muscles in her face and jaw softened. Her forehead unknitted and her vision turned inward.

The darkness of her closed eyes twisted and moved. The blackness became misty, the mist formed shapes, soft and difficult to make out at first and then firmer and clearer.

She saw the family she had once known. The images she had of her family were eight years old now. That was such a long time ago. She had just a few images of three people that lived inside a peapod deep in her mind. She had no good use for these images, often it was painful to allow them to come forth, sometimes they were comforting, but they never helped her to do the things she needed to do.

There was a man, large but rather soft, like an older bear. His clothes were soft too and smelled of coffee and often of food. His large hands were clumsy but kind. He often spilled food on himself. He was never quite fully shaved no matter how recently he had tried, it lent a bluish tint to his face.

A woman, quite tall and athletic; like a hare, somewhat anxious and very sincere. She had neat, shoulder length hair and a surprisingly loud laugh. Sometimes she smelled of perfume. Often she smelled of ink.

And a small boy, younger than her but not by much. He was small for his age perhaps though he had lovely large eyes and he looked at her with trust and curiosity equally mixed. He followed her as best he could. His near constant attention was wonderful and simultaneously irksome.

Sometimes she remembered some words and phrases. Bits of conversation and the sounds of names drifted into her consciousness; and sensations, hugs and hand-holding and the way a smile on someone else's lips can powerfully change how another person feels.

They were images she had no use for, or so she thought, but they refused to disappear completely and as long as they stayed mostly in their peapod deep inside her, emerging only on nights like this one and sometimes in the images cast on the wall of her cave by evening fire light, then she would allow them some visiting time when it was safe to do so. For reasons she could not understand she felt it was right to do this.

She fell asleep like that, memories and dreams mixing together.

The next day she set off again, west towards the border with Laos. Again the road was uphill. The villages thinned out and there was only forest and road. The sky was dark and she knew it would rain later.

Before she reached an official border crossing she abandoned the motorbike. She would miss it but she would not allow herself that luxury for long.

She always avoided official borders. Border towns tended to be tough and dangerous and to involve unnecessary delay and violence. She did not need to use false documents and lies to cross between countries. To her all documents were false and pointless and all borders just the same, equally empty of real meaning.

It was impossible to police a complete border or build a wall around a whole country and if you could survive in a jungle or a forest or live well in the mountains you could cross between many countries as easily as the animals do.

It started to rain. A sudden and heavy downpour. She kept moving just as if nothing had changed. She had a two-day walk through the dense trees ahead of her. She would need to build a more robust shelter that night. That was all the significance the rain held; that and the leeches would be more active. The leeches hid under the lower leaves of the grasses and when they felt an animal brush past they dropped and tried to attach to whatever was passing. Their bite was painless and they even injected a chemical to help the blood flow freely so they could have a good meal. When their meal was done they would drop off and return to a place on the underside of a leaf to digest and wait. They were not the worst sort of creature. She had seen worse. She had met worse and she had killed worse.

She would not know when exactly she entered Laos but she knew exactly where she was headed. It was the place that had been the closest thing to what she could call home for more than half her life- a place that was familiar but sometimes less than warm.

She had one more night of being free- free to be whatever strange hybrid thing she was. Free not to have to define herself. Not having to fit in to the strict and harsh regime that had made her strong but kept her bound.

*Chapter 3*


Eight years earlier:


"Everything is coming up Burnham," Marcus Burnham thought to himself as he stood on the front lawn of his gorgeous new family home in Tolbundle Bridge in the county of Dorset, in the south of England with a fresh glass of Prosecco bubbling cheerfully in his hand.


It was, in his opinion, the very nicest house, in the very prettiest town, in the very best part of England and possibly the world.


Marcus said that short, silly phrase; "Everything is coming up Burnham" to himself when he was happy and he knew it and lately things were going so well for the Burnham family that he was often really very happy indeed. More than at any other time in his life, things were going his way.


It was a particularly sunny afternoon in May and he was watching his two children, Ellie (short for Eleanor) and Tristan playing on their trampoline. It was a neat little trampoline, built into a hollow in the lawn and Marcus loved to watch his children playing together on it.

The Burnham family had just moved from London to this big house in a small town in rural Dorset. Marcus was a lawyer and worked at a firm in London but he was originally from Dorset and had always wanted to move back. His wife Harriet was also a lawyer. She was a born and bred Londoner but had wanted to move out of London almost as soon as their first child had been born.

Marcus had met Harriet very soon after he left college and got his first job in London. They were working at the same firm, at the same low level, doing all the jobs the more senior people didn't want to do.

They worked together and socialized together. Marcus had been attracted to Harriet from the start. She was smart, funny and kind. They made a slightly unlikely couple, viewed from the outside, him a big clumsy good natured chap who, no matter how hard he tried, always looked a little like a large pile of laundry needing to be done and her, alert, neat and very much 'together'.

She had been quite a successful school gymnast before she grew too tall, whereas Marcus had played a bit as a prop forward for his school rugby team but was never very good.

She always seemed to be in control whereas Marcus was forever losing things and forgetting appointments.

The fact was, however, that together they worked. They felt comfortable and happy in each other's company and when they looked at one another they both felt that unmistakable connection that Harriet uncharacteristically described as "hubba, hubba, hubba" on what was officially their fourth date.

They both worked hard and bought a house they couldn't afford in a nice part of London. They continued to work hard and after a time and moves up the legal ladder they could afford the house. They got married in a registry office and celebrated with a dinner with their families and friends in a Cuban restaurant in Whitechapel. It was nothing too fancy but it was a warm and friendly day that they both remembered with joy.

Three years later their first child Eleanor was born. They started talking about moving out of London "someday" then. When their second child, a boy they named Tristan, was born a year later they started to make practical arrangements to move to the countryside.

It took longer than they hoped to find a buyer for their house in London and a place in Dorset that they wanted, and could afford, to move to.

When they found Tolbundle Bridge and the large but cosy house for sale on the edge of the village with its own orchard, large front lawn and enough space to let an army of children roam free, they couldn't believe their luck.

Since they had moved Harriet and Marcus truly believed they had found the perfect place for them and their family; the place that they would call home forever.

Marcus still had to get the train to London from Dorchester four or five times a week while Harriet worked from home but the sacrifice was more than worth the return. They both loved the idea that their children would grow up in a place like this. They wanted them to have a free, relaxed childhood.

Ellie was five and Tristan was four, it was time for them to be starting school but before that Marcus had something big planned. They were all going on holiday for a whole year. More than a holiday, this would be a proper adventure. They would travel through China, Laos, Cambodia, Thailand, Malaysia, Indonesia, Australia, New Zealand, Brazil, Mexico, America and then back to England. That was why Marcus was, if anything, extra happy today, thinking of the experiences they would share on what would be, genuinely, the trip of a lifetime.

Harriet and Marcus had spent many lovely evening hours with a glass of wine each pouring over maps and reading travel guides planning this great adventure for the whole family and now it was nearly upon them. Marcus could not have been more excited if he had been a child himself, and in some ways he was.

If this meant that the children would start school a bit late so be it. Ellie was very advanced in reading and maths for her age and Marcus and Harriet believed kids in England started school too young anyway. They had done their research and it seemed that in countries where kids started school as late as seven years old, the standard of educational results were often higher than in England. The experiences they would gain on the journey would help to form them as open-minded and curious individuals and citizens of the world for life.

It had also been a struggle for Harriet and Marcus to get the time off from their jobs but they had fought for it. Life was for living and they intended to do so. They were not going to miss out on their children's formative years. Harriet had been educated largely at a boarding school and while it had not been a terrible experience, she was just as determined as Marcus to spend as much time as possible with Ellie and Tristan as they grew.

Over a number of months they prepared the kids for the trip in what they hoped was a fun way. They ate (very mild) Thai and Malaysian curries, learned about the Maori culture of New Zealand (which had to be edited because in contained a lot of war and violence), learned about the animals and plants of all the countries they would visit.

Tristan was particularly taken with one species of very large bat that lived in Thailand and Malaysia and Ellie nicknamed him 'The Big Bat' because of that.

They even learned little bits of the languages they would encounter- mostly "please" and "thank you" because it is always good to be polite but also any other phrases they could pick up and remember. The children loved to learn the names of food items and animals in the various languages.

'Jugo' was 'juice' in Spanish; 'crisps' were 'Shû piàn' in Chinese (they thought) and 'hamburger' was 'hamburger' in Malay.

Ellie liked the words 'jacaré' which meant 'alligator' in Portuguese and 'ngū' which meant ''snake' in Thai. The Thai language used a completely different alphabet that looked like abstract and possibly magical symbols. She also liked dangerous animals.

Tristan especially liked 'kaka' which was 'parrot' in Maori.

Harriet and Marcus fretted more over useful and practical phrases. Marcus sometimes woke at night with a great sense of the responsibility he had for the welfare of his family. It would start with concerns about keeping them safe on the trip, then quickly he would be concerned about keeping them safe in general. Would he be up to the task? How could he know? Well, he would do his best. That idea seemed too flimsy and commonplace but it was all he had, all anyone had in the end.

Marcus and Harriet could not have been more proud of their children; clever, fit and kind as they were. They knew that they were living every bit as well as anyone could hope to and they were grateful for their happiness. When they returned from their trip they might even get a dog.

Of course, Marcus, who was inclined towards worry, sometimes feared that their lives were too happy now to remain so. Something inside him warned that nothing so good could last forever, or even, perhaps, for very long. His wife and two children; when he watched them going about their normal, daily routines, made pictures, like paintings or even short films made up only of small scenes with no plot; just a present with no past and a future hopeful and frightening in equal amounts because it was completely unknown, made his heart beat faster with pride, hope and anxiety, filled him with love, deep, serious and joyous; but the shadow of that love was fear and it would always be there.

"Lunch everyone," Harriet called from the kitchen, "Come and get it."

The children came running as Marcus put his arm around his wife and they went inside together.

Chapter 4

The Burnhams were still in the first month of their great adventure. In fact they were just beginning to become accustomed to this new, footloose sort of life; one in which they could stay or go on a whim, or a family vote. If they liked a hotel they were staying in particularly well they could remain there as long as felt right, if they were not having fun, they could pack up and move on with no trouble.

It is not as easy to be free as we hope; it is quite usual to miss the structure of work and school, social appointments and even visits to the dentist, but the Burnhams were now becoming good at freedom and they had lots of time left to practise; which made for a very pleasant feeling, like when you wake up early and think you have to go to school then realize it's Saturday and you can stay in bed as long as you like and can even go back to sleep at your leisure.

It was late morning. The day was filling up like a balloon with the sort of heat and light that is never experienced in England; the sort of heat and light that gently gets under your skin and loosens and relaxes every part of you. It produces in you a relaxed energy that you can enjoy just for itself, perhaps sunbathing with a book, or you can bring it to anything you need or want to do and you will find you are happier doing it and probably do it better too.

Ellie sat on the beach looking at the place where the sea met the sky. She could see the exact line. It seemed very far away and very interesting. For some reason it felt to Ellie that it would be wonderful and important to find and explore that place. She would at least have liked a closer look at that spot where the sea and the sky seemed to gently come together but it seemed so very far away and she was not that good at swimming, yet. She practised her swimming all the time. She was very comfortable in the water and though she was not a very fast swimmer she was strong and steady, she could carry an easy breaststroke for a very long time; and she was always getting better.

She looked up and down the beach. At the end of the beach the forest began. It went like this- sand, sand, sand, trees. Just like the sea and the sky; or, at least, very much like; a place where two different worlds met, but it was not nearly so far away. She got up and trotted off to have a look.

Just inside the line of the forest there was so much life to see. The ground was covered in a thick carpet of rotting leaves and out of them life burst up violently. Lizards, ants, spiders, small rodents. Some bigger rodents moved about in there, probably some snakes too.

And there were mushrooms of all kinds; big, small, brown, grey, white, round, long and curved like tubes- a whole gallery of fungi; yet another world, complete in itself. There was one great big mushroom that stood out. The first thing Ellie noticed was its colour. It was the strangest colour. It was almost purple but not quite. It looked like something from a comic or a storybook. It was almost shiny because of its extremely smooth surface. That was another remarkable thing about it, all the other mushrooms had rough, nobbled and scored surfaces but this one was uniquely smooth. It was the same sort of shape as half a football or a particular type of umbrella, the kind that slopes down to your shoulders and creates a helmet around your head to keep the rain off.

There was something fascinating and otherworldly about it. Ellie's attention became focused entirely on it, she was drawn towards it but she approached it carefully, as if it might jump at her like a big spider had done just a couple of days before. It didn't.

She knelt down to have a closer look, her finger instinctively inching forward to touch it, and as she scrutinized it there was a sudden little explosion and a cloud of something very light, not much denser than the air itself but different and very powerful.

She was there; then she was gone.

Harriet was the first to notice. A moment of uncertainty, of thinking she must be around somewhere close by, that she would reappear any moment now; calling her name, at first softly and then more and more powerfully calling, the beginning of panic, and then panic full blown.

She called for Marcus who was playing in small breaking waves at the shoreline with Tristan. He picked Tristan up and came running.

A long nightmare was beginning.

Chapter 5

She was there; then she was somewhere else entirely.

Ellie opened her eyes into near complete darkness. At first she could see nothing; she might as well have been wearing a blindfold. She could smell something though, a damp smell that was very strong and all around her, wrapping her up like a horrid blanket; and she could hear something, water dripping, water dripping in lots of different places, all around her. It was cold, suddenly very cold compared to the beach. She hugged herself unconsciously in an attempt to stay warm; it had very little effect.

She raised a hand and moved it though the space around her until it found a wall. There was a little rivulet of water running down it. The surface of the wall was a soft, claylike, natural material. She leant on it with both hands and tried to stand up. She got her feet under her and slowly lifted herself up. She felt dizzy and almost immediately fell down again.

The ground was softer than she had feared in that moment of falling. She tried once more to stand up but she became just as dizzy and felt just as weak and so she fell again.

She sat there and took some deep breaths. She thought of her mother with a sudden longing that was stronger than any feeling she had ever felt. Thinking of her Mum now, she suddenly felt like crying. She wanted to cry out for her as she always did when he was really afraid; and she was more afraid now than she had ever been, but no sound emerged when she opened her mouth no matter how hard she tried. She couldn't control her balance, her limbs. Now, it seemed, even her speech had abandoned her.

She waited. It took several minutes but she began to feel her strength return to her. She put both her hands on the wall once again. She braced herself and screwed up her courage and she slowly got herself on her feet.

She was steadier now. She turned slowly and braced her back against the wall. She stayed there a long time; how long she didn't really know. Her eyes began slowly to adjust to the darkness around her and she got a clearer sense of the sort of place she found herself in.

It was a cave. A vast cave with no beginning or end that she could see. Despite its size it was a 'closing in' that she felt not an opening up. She looked all around but could see no obvious way out. No matter how large a trap is, it is still a trap.

As she scanned the walls for a way to escape she noticed that they were textured in a striking way. There were patterns there that drew her eye. The walls were covered in pictures; dark, simple pictures on the lighter brown surface of the cave walls. As she focused on them they began to stand out and make themselves known.

The pictures were of all sorts of animals- deer, cattle, boar, dogs of many shapes and sizes, wolves, jackals, hyena, cats (big and small), elephants, rodents, giraffe, monkeys, and porcupines. All the animals she had ever seen in real life, in books or on television and many more.

Maybe some of them didn't exist any longer or had never truly existed, they might be storybook animals.

As her eyes focused and became more and more accustomed to the light she understood that almost every inch of the cave was covered in these pictures and always animals; no people, no buildings, were depicted. There was nothing of the human world here. She felt afraid to make a noise.

She felt like something or 'somethings' were out there in the blackness and although she had no idea what they might be she definitely didn't want to meet them. It was exactly as if there was an invisible force pinning her against the wall.

She felt, in short, exactly like what she was, a small child, afraid and alone.

Time ticked by slowly, or stood stock still, it was the same thing in this place.

After many minutes she realised, somewhere deep down inside her, that she had to move. She had to do something. She could not just stay where she was, passively waiting for something to happen to her. She needed to do anything she could to find her way back to her family.

Slowly..

she..

moved..

forward..

..and at that moment she was hit by something fast and powerful. Suddenly the cave was illuminated with the light of a number of flaming torches attached to the walls, the walls that were bare, brown clay now; all the pictures were suddenly gone. The walls had been wiped clean in an instant; and Ellie was surrounded.

The smell, the energy, the mass of the large group of animals around her was overpowering. She could hardly breathe but the sound of their breathing was massive.

Their eyes glowed in the light from the torches. Without being touched she was pushed back to the wall by the sheer force of their presence.

One of the creatures moved forward towards Ellie. It was massive, covered in fur that looked dirty but was actually an intimidating mixture of brown and black. It walked on four legs. It was much bigger in its front end than its rear. Its hips were relatively very small and tucked under. It looked something like a misshapen giant dog with horrifyingly over-sized and powerful jaws.

It lowered its head towards Ellie. Its mouth was open, tasting the air with its tongue. Streams of saliva dripped from teeth evolved perfectly for crushing the bones of large animals. The muscles of its massive head and neck looked strong enough to push those incredible jaws through the task of smashing anything it chose. Its breath smelt of rotting flesh.

The great nose touched Ellie on the forehead and she felt her stomach turn inside out. The whole world spun and Ellie collapsed into unconsciousness. The last thing she remembered was a sound that was something like a high-pitched laugh but not cruel. There was something just a little soft about it.

Chapter 6

Once again Ellie was in a strange place. It was warm this time and she was lying on some sort of soft bedding, very soft indeed. She couldn't tell what sort of material it was. It was not like any she had felt at home. If it was like anything she recognized, it was like leaves or something to do with a forest floor but it was dry and warm and woven and pleasant to be on. It was comforting despite her fear and loneliness and, she noticed suddenly, her extreme hunger.

The matting somehow provided just enough reassurance to stop her from breaking down in tears- somewhere inside her she believed that whoever had provided this bedding was unlikely to wish her nothing but harm.

She was famished, she was confused, she was exhausted but mostly she was sad. She knew that she was surely somewhere very far away from her family now.

She had a deep feeling of being lost and alone in a big, big world. Despite how very young she was, she understood that the rules had changed.

At the same time she understood that this was not some accident; someone had done this to her and so much depended on who that person was and what they wanted from her.

She seemed to be alone but she knew that if she tried to leave this place, wherever and whatever it was, she would be stopped. She had yet to meet her captor and who was to say that things would not get worse when she did. She couldn't see any sign of who was to blame for all this but she felt their presence as powerfully as if it were a smell hanging in the air; a deep, animal smell.

She looked around. A cave again. This time a smaller one, altogether cosier than the first. If that first cave had been a grand hall, this one was a child's bedroom, one that had been prepared in advance for her.

Her eyes went to the walls of the cave, looking for pictures like the ones she had seen before. She could see nothing there. There were also no little streams of water running down them and there was no smell of damp. In fact, there was a slight scent of flowers in the air around her; flowers and animal. It was not a bad smell, it was a smell that was fresh and alive.

She could see what looked like an exit covered with a woven blanket. No light leaked through from outside. She could hear the sounds of small creatures, mice or something similar, moving about invisibly around her. The sounds made her feel even more unnerved.

She imagined that outside there would just be more cave and if she got out of the caves where would she be then. She felt completely helpless; but she had to do something. It was an exhausting feeling.

After some time of frustrated indecision she worked up the courage and energy to begin to make her way towards the possible exit.

As soon as she did so a creature emerged from behind the blanket. It was not hurried; it seemed as if it had just happened to be entering at that moment. It looked like a giant rabbit. It had the most amazingly long ears with beautiful black tips. It approached her with an awkward hop and step motion. Its back legs were too big for its front legs causing it to move as if it were constantly falling forward and just catching its balance at the end of each step.

"Don't be afraid little girl," the creature said. "You are safe now."

The creature touched the girl on her tiny shoulder. "For now all you need is to eat, sleep, play and grow strong."

There was something comforting about the creature despite its strangeness and size. It had an air of gentleness about it. It reached out a large paw that contained a bowl.

"Eat this, it will be good for you."

Ellie stared at the bowl. It contained a dried brown substance. It smelled slightly sweet and she heard her stomach gurgle as if to tell her it was good. She took it and moved away. The creature did not follow her.

She took a little of the food and put it in her mouth. It tasted good. She ate. The more she ate the more hungry she realised she had been.

As she ate her fear diminished. She felt more and more relaxed and before she could finish the whole serving she had fallen, once again, into a deep sleep.

Chapter 7

The training began long before Ellie realised she was being trained at all. The training was her life because what you do all the time becomes who you are.

Her only companions at first were the giant Hare creature and the birds and the beasts that lived in the wilderness all around her- from tiny insects to the giant monitor lizards that fed on them and almost everything else that didn't run away fast enough and soon enough.

With the fierce curiosity of a very young child she made an unconscious study of the ways of all these creatures. She paid minute attention to the ways in which they interacted within their own species and with other species. She saw how they preyed on each other and yet depended on each other.

She spoke to the animals sometimes though she understood that this was not the best way to communicate with them, they had their own wordless ways of communication. She could not have explained of course why she did this. She was simply compelled to do so; driven by a need for more and more connection.

Ellie felt first hand the harshness of nature. She had to learn to deal with the days when it was too hot and she found herself panting like a dog. She had to learn how to cope with nights when it was so cold that the shivering became her whole being.

Outside the cave, or system of caves, in which she now lived the wilderness was her whole world. The mouth of the cave system emerged near the edge of a large forest. The forest itself was of a shade of green so thick and so dark that only the work of a thousand years could have created it.

Next to the forest was a flat plain of what probably used to be fields, long uncultivated, burned brown by the sun and beyond that a small lake. Only the birds could see the whole area as one piece and they had concerns other than the making of mental maps to occupy their time what with raising their chicks and noisily guarding their territories.

There had been a time when the fields were used for farming but that was long ago. The nearest people; and they did not live anywhere that could be seriously considered near, would tell you directly that the forest was haunted.

More than one hundred years ago strange and bad things had begun happening in and around those woods. People disappeared amongst these tall and densely packed trees and some came out of the trees no longer the same person they went in and no longer in their right minds- telling tales of something like the ghosts of animals, the angry ghosts of animals- enormous, fierce and revengeful.

Domestic animals disappeared; not killed by wild animals, as must be expected to sometimes happen as a price the world will exact from the farmer. No corpses were discovered; they simply went missing and could not be found. Assuming they were somewhere in the forest, not many wished to try to find them.

The grandchildren and great grandchildren of the ones who had left the place still knew it and called it "The Forest of Bad Dreams". It featured in many exciting and frightening stories told in the villages and towns. The area was a sort of myth now, only visited in the imagination and safer kept that way.

Maybe once in many years a brave young person seeking adventure would come in search of the mysterious place. They didn't find adventure. First they found a cold and hollow feeling in their bones. If they had the good sense to heed the warning this feeling carried they left and that was all they found. If they were foolish, or a little too brave for their own well being, they found terror and were very lucky indeed if they also found their way home again broken and more timid.

As the place was bad for humans; it was good for every other animal and it became as wild a place as there has ever been.

This was all, of course, in a country with a name and a history and politics and art and culture; but Ellie knew not one thing about those matters and the life she led and the company she kept did not recognise or acknowledge such paper-thin ideas.

She spent most of her days outside. She was always moving. She grew strong beyond her years.

Ellie adapted to her new world. She had to. The Hare was a gentle mentor and a patient teacher. He spoke to her all the time, teaching her the names of some the plants and animals around her but in a relaxed and unstructured manner. He often corrected little things about the way she stood or the way she moved. Gently but firmly he would say:

"Brace yourself like this before you jump little thing and feel the power coming from here in your hips and the back of your legs. You'll go further, be stronger and won't hurt yourself when you land."

The Hare was at his most specific and serious when talking about these details of movement.

The only time that the Hare would lose his patience with Ellie was when she climbed trees- and she loved to climb trees. She loved the feeling of her muscles working; her hands and feet gripping as she steadily rose towards the sky. She loved the feeling of sitting near the tips of one of the larger tress and sharing the view of the birds. She felt happy and peaceful there, tired from the effort of reaching the peak and relaxing in the breeze in a place that somehow seemed perfect in itself.

The Hare could not climb trees and his job was partly to keep Ellie safe. When she dashed off to climb a giant tree he would call after her to come down. When she ignored him he would try to remain calm and poised but his jaw would develop a slight twitch and then clench in a manner it was difficult for him to control and embarrassing for him to acknowledge and he would fuss internally all the time until she came down to earth again safely.

On those occasions it was not unknown for Ellie to receive a sharp blow to the ear with one of the Hare's fore paws.

That did little to discourage Ellie though. Her outdoor, active life was building her into a tough little creature, used to falls, knock and bruises and the Hare's heart was not in the blow. His heart had melted to the child early on; more than it should have.

Every day she ate a bowl of the same sweet brown dried mushrooms in the evening and her memories of her family retreated a little further into the deepest caves of her memories. It was soon almost exclusively in her dreams that she saw her family; her mother, father and brother and just who exactly they were and why these dreams hurt her heart so much and sometimes found her crying when she woke became harder and harder for her to understand.

She naturally came to wish for these dreams to go, to vanish for good but they kept coming, from time to time, confusing her and disturbing her otherwise settled and ordered existence.

More than two years passed like this, with the Hare gently helping her to grow strong, before she met the Ape.

Chapter 8

Every evening the Hare disappeared. He didn't just leave Ellie. He was nowhere to be found.

He brought Ellie back to her sleeping quarters and when he passed through the woven blanket that served as her door he vanished.

Once Ellie had tried to follow him but emerging through the doorway only moments after him she found that he had disappeared as if he had been a ghost. She asked him about this the next day but all he would say was that it was not time to talk about such things. Ellie could sense that no more information would be given on the subject and so she accepted it, for the moment, as a mystery whose solution might be revealed to her at some later date.

Every morning Ellie awoke ravenous and every morning the Hare brought her breakfast. His step, although it looked awkward when he moved slowly, was light and sometimes she did not hear him approach. His large fuzzy head would simply appear in the entrance-way. He would blink his big eyes and that gesture carried within it all the warmth of a smile.

He would come just before dawn so Ellie thought of him a little like the sunrise; a smiling sunrise who, best of all, brought food.

It was a pleasant ritual, a reassuring way to greet each new day.

Then one morning, as she rose, Ellie heard something that sounded like a large boulder rolling through the caves towards her quarters, a sound like ten big storms approaching all at once and in a hurry.

This rumble that was headed towards her was clearly not the Hare. It grew louder and more threatening as it came closer; a powerful, intimidating and commanding noise.

Ellie unconsciously prepared for trouble in the way the Hare had taught her. She dropped her stance a little and consciously softened the tension in her knees and ankles despite her growing anxiety. She screwed the soles of her feet outwards into the earth, breathed in deeply and then not quite fully out, bracing her stomach to support her back. She was preparing for danger.

The din grew and Ellie concentrated on controlling her breathing, staying calm. Along with the noise she could now detect a smell, a smell as big as the noise. They mingled together into one terrific sensation of approaching power. This was like no animal Ellie had yet encountered. Most creatures tried to move more or less secretly but this beast clearly had no concern about whoever or whatever might hear it coming. This was a creature accustomed to being made way for.

Ellie concentrated on the entrance, ready to deal with whatever came through it but wishing whatever it was that she could hear and smell would pass her by or that the Hare would appear somehow to support her. The seconds passed like hours as she tried to control the monsters her imagination was creating.

Then a huge dark ball of muscle and movement burst into her little alcove and she almost fell over from the sheer force of its presence.

It came out of the blur of motion and to an abrupt stop in an instant. Then it slowly unfolded before her.

Like the Hare, the Ape was a giant but a much more frightening one. He most resembled a gorilla but no gorilla was ever this large. He was at least seven feet tall and almost impossibly muscular. His body seemed supernaturally strong. It was mostly covered in black fur but he had a strange orange tint to his beard. His eyes were a mesmerizingly intense golden brown.

The giant took a massive breath and the small room seemed to shake. Ellie saw his canine teeth for the first time, like daggers of ivory. It took all she had for Ellie to stand her ground and face him, unsure as she was in that moment of what would happen next.

"Well," his voice was so deep Ellie felt it down in her insides, "At least you stayed on your feet, …just about."

"Where is…?" Ellie started to ask, in a voice which betrayed her fear far more clearly than she had hoped.

Before she could finish the Ape leapt across the room faster than her eyes could follow. In one giant move he was on her and she was in his massive grasp, her feet dangling helplessly in the air. She felt no bigger or more substantial than a blade of grass. The golden brown eyes burned into her with an intensity she was not accustomed to experiencing with the Hare. He scanned her from top to bottom, some private calculations going on his mind. It was as if he was trying to fit her to some task in his imagination.

Under his breath she heard him say something that was probably-

"So small." But she couldn't be sure.

The look on his face suggested that he was far from convinced that Ellie would be up to whatever secret task he had in mind for her.

"Not here today," the Ape replied when he eventually spoke aloud, "Today you will work with me."

When he saw a tear welling up in the girl's eye he added-

"You will see the Hare again soon but today you begin the work that you must do with me."

It was the first time Ellie had heard the word 'work' and the way things worked with the Ape were very different from with the Hare. He was the one who started Ellie learning all the human skills she would need. He taught her to read and write; he introduced her to the sciences and began the process of preparing her to deal with (and disguise herself within) the human world. He began the strange and complex process of teaching her to disguise herself as what, in truth, she was, or should have been- a young human being.

The first week they worked alone. The atmosphere was colder, less friendly than Ellie had enjoyed with the Hare. The Ape was stern in general, there was always something in his manner to suggest that she was letting him down, failing to come up to some measure she couldn't understand because it was never made clear to her.

They started every day in a new room in the caves, a sort of study. Somehow the Ape had stocked it with all sorts of books and maps and later even basic laboratory equipment. The Ape was surprisingly deft with his massive hands. Ellie remained fascinated forever by the sight of his powerful hands; digits that she would see tear down small trees just to work out some minor frustration later turning the pages of a book with patience and care.

The Ape instituted a set programme of exercise every morning after breakfast. After that he brought her to the study and they started the day's lesson.

After the formal lessons they went out into the world and the Ape would give her practical demonstrations and illustrations of the abstract facts and ideas she had been exposed to that morning. It was a system that worked well but which was very demanding for a child, there was no time off, and it left Ellie exhausted at the end of every day.

On the day when he first introduced Ellie to the concept of 'Levers' for example, the Ape took her into the forest and showed her a large rock.

"Pick it up." The Ape said.

Ellie tried. She strained and pulled and gritted her teeth and after much effort, the rock had not moved even an inch.

"Try again."

The Ape pointed and adopted his sternest tone.

Ellie did. She was nothing if not determined.

She redoubled her efforts. She strained every muscle, she used all the knowledge the Hare had given her as to how to maximise the power she could exert on this frustratingly fixed object.

It sat there unmoved like a lazy toad. Ellie was covered in sweat and already aching.

The Ape grunted.

"Wait."

He strode to a nearby small tree. He fixed it with a stare for a moment and then took it in his grip. The muscles of his back contracted with his near impossible strength and the tree came up in his hands. From it he ripped a good large branch. He threw it at Ellie's feet.

Then he brought a smaller rock and dropped it near the branch.

"Move the large rock."

Ellie considered for a moment and then, recalling the morning's lesson, she placed the small rock near the large one, put one end of the branch under the base of the large one, rested the branch on the smaller and pushed down with all her might on the far end which was sitting up in the air by now like one end of a see-saw.

It took all she had, and the rock did not rise by much, but it rose, slowly and only a little, but it rose and she held in there for a moment or two, stronger than she had ever been.

She turned to smile at the Ape and the rock fell.

The Ape grunted.

"Come here."

Ellie thought she might be in line for some praise, perhaps a pleasant pat on the head- something so rarely received from the Ape as to be very, very special and desired.

Instead the Ape picked her up and threw her to the ground. He crouched above her and growled.

"Protect yourself," he roared. The sight of his gleaming, white, sword-like canines threatened to freeze Ellie's mind.

She pushed her knees between herself and the Ape.

"Make an angle," the Ape demanded.

Ellie, in a panic, shifted her hips to one side.

"Grip my arm with your legs, the hips above my elbow."

Ellie did as she was instructed.

"Grip my wrist, push your hips forward with all your might."

Ellie did so.

"Good, you may stop," the Ape's tone was soft again, as soft as he ever was.

Ellie; however, did not stop. She suddenly felt she may be winning in some impossible manner and she was angry at being manipulated and ordered about. It was time for her to get some revenge.

She put all her strength into a genuine attempt to snap the Ape's arm at the elbow.

It didn't work.

The Ape stood and bent his arm with ease. He slowly lifted Ellie until she was looking him in the eyes. The strange, golden eyes stared deep into her and he smiled, showing the terrifying teeth again.

"Cherish that feeling, fighter. Keep it safe for when you need it."

From that day on Ellie and the Ape fought regularly. Of course, it was a great fight for Ellie but little for the Ape. He pushed her very hard but seldom injured her. When injuries did happen he showed her how to treat them.

They made liniments for minor injuries from plants like Rhubarb, Gardenia, Safflower, Frankincense and Myrrh.

When injuries were more serious, as they seldom but sometimes were, those times when an injury would not heal and the Ape was concerned that Ellie may have sustained damage to a tendon or ligament, perhaps even damage to a bone, they would make a poultice, a thick muddy pack of herbs in raw egg.

These poultices were made from a small amount of the poison Aconite, with Magnolia root, Costus Root, Fennel, Cinnamon Bark, Rosebud Bark, Teasel Root and other plants from the garden that the Ape kept as his own Chemist's shop and to instruct Ellie in the ways of plants in a more formal and technical manner than the Hare had done up until now.

Ellie was guided in how to produce these medicines by the Ape but she had to do the work herself. If she didn't do the work, she would not get the medicine.

For small cuts and nosebleeds she would wrap a thin strip of root around her hand just below the knuckles, pull it tight and squeeze her fist hard.

As time passed Ellie hardened physically and mentally and she could see that the Ape was pleased with her progress although he never said so outright.

He taught her not to be intimidated by pain but to think clearly and take appropriate action.

After the first week or so the Hare had returned as the Ape had promised. He treated her as he always had but now the Ape was always there too. The presence of the Ape made everything more serious.

The Ape was work embodied.

The Ape had a way of walking on his squat back legs with his paws crossed behind his back, a little like an old man in deep thought, that Ellie came to unconsciously copy until one day when the Hare pointed it out to the Ape and she was ordered to stop it immediately.

Chapter 9

The next teacher to enter Ellie's life was the Crocodile. She was becoming somewhat used to fantastic creatures and she was well acquainted with large lizards from observing the giant Monitor lizards that lived nearby but she was still astonished by the length of this beast. Its tail could not get all the way into her sleeping quarters while its head and body were inside.

From the first moment that she saw the Crocodile until the very last Ellie always got the impression that she was about to be eaten. There was never an easy moment when she didn't expect those jaws to snap her up and twist her to pieces before rising up and lowering her down the huge throat.

"Follow me and do not speak," were the first words the Crocodile said and then she immediately turned and started out of the caves. Ellie jogged along behind her obediently.

They went straight to the lake. The Crocodile never once looking back to check on Ellie. When they arrived she spoke without turning her head.

"Get on my back," she commanded.

Ellie was confused and unsure. She was accustomed to the fact that her teachers were dignified creatures and was not exactly in the habit of playing piggyback with them. Also the Crocodile's back looked cold and hard and particularly uninviting but she did as she was told.

"Hold on," Continued the hard, grey monster and then she slowly and smoothly slipped into the water of the lake.

The water was so cold that Ellie found it difficult to breathe for a minute. Her lungs felt like they had frozen solid within her chest.

"Breathe in deeply, do not breathe out fully, form a picture in your mind of fire." The Crocodile instructed.

Ellie attempted to do as she was told. Her skin tingled and she began to feel light-headed. It was not a pleasant feeling but she persisted.

It began to be difficult to hold onto the great leathery back. Its surface was so hard and unforgiving. She was glad of the grip strength she had developed from climbing so many trees. She almost smiled as she thought of the Hare, the very opposite of the Crocodile, but there was no time for pining after soft things now.

She concentrated hard, held tight and tried to breathe in the way the crocodile had told her.

She attempted to form an image of burning flames in her mind's eye but it was not easy as the cold water ran over her legs and arms and made her shiver violently.

Ellie squeezed her eyes tightly shut and removed her mind from the pain in her hands, wrists, feet and ankles. She continued with the fire breathing and slowly she felt as if her skin was growing harder, becoming like a sort of armour, a sort of crocodile skin and she started to feel somewhat in control of her body.

She could open her lungs without gasping and struggling and feeling as if someone were gripping the lower ends of her diaphragm and twisting cruelly. She no longer felt like there was a giant weight relentlessly pressing down on her stomach.

Then the Crocodile, without the slightest warning, dived below the surface of the water. Ellie became aware of what was happening only just in time to take in a deep and desperate gulp of air and hold it.

The Crocodile plunged down deeper and Ellie held onto that breath. Almost immediately she felt that she needed to get to the surface or she was doomed.

She might disappoint the Crocodile, she might be failing some kind of test, she might have quite a long swim back to shore, she might be punished; this teacher seemed like the sort who would think nothing of beating her, but it was time to get up to the surface again. Nothing else was as important. This was a matter of life and death; any consequences could be dealt with afterwards.

She let go of the Crocodile's back, her greatly taxed arms and legs thanking her for the relief, and pushed upwards towards the light and the air with all the might she had remaining.

At that same moment she felt herself wrapped in a tight embrace. She was confused, she pushed harder but went nowhere. She looked down and saw that the Crocodile's tail was tightly coiled around her middle like a huge snake. In terror she realised that she could not free herself.

She could not struggle. She had no chance to break the grip of this giant brute. She had to try to relax. She had to try to slow her heart rate. Fighting would only make the end come sooner. She had to…

She suddenly realised she was dying.

The urge to panic was immediate and overwhelming. She beat and pulled at the tail that held her despite knowing so well it was pointless. She would have bitten into it if she could have reached it with her teeth. Even if she could not save herself perhaps she could hurt the Crocodile even a little. She hated this creature, she hated her strength, coldness and cruelty. She hated that the Crocodile would surely care not one bit for all the hatred Ellie could possibly muster.

For a moment she felt sad as this seemed such a pointless and sudden way to die and then she was gone.

When she came back to consciousness she was on the shore by the lake. The Hare and the Ape were there as well as the Crocodile. The Hare looked concerned and the Ape looked angry but the look was not directed at her but rather at the great reptile.

They were arguing. She had never seen the Hare and the Ape argue.

"Not good enough." The Crocodile was saying with impatience in her voice.

"You need to go slower, you need to be more gentle." The Hare explained.

"They learn slowly, they grow slowly," the Ape continued, "But they learn well. They are adaptable, amazing in the variety of things they learn to turn those remarkable hands to."

"They learn too slowly," the Crocodile hissed, "She wastes my time."

Ellie lay still, pulling all the air she could into her frozen, soaked and aching body. Her three teachers continued as if she were not even there.

Despite all this the Crocodile came almost every day and taught Ellie to take more and more control of her breathing. The Crocodile herself could hold her breathe for what seemed like forever. She could slow her heart rate down so dramatically that it seemed that it was not necessary for it to beat at all.

Ellie's sessions with the Crocodile were short and intense. They left her light-headed and confused but the length of time she could hold her breath for was slowly expanding along with the capacity of her lungs.

The Crocodile taught Ellie to raise her heart rate when she needed to become more alert, when she needed to be ready for action.

The technique involved breathing in deeply using the muscles of her stomach to really open her lungs, then out but not all the way. Ellie would draw her breath back in strongly and breathe out once again, continuing as she started to feel her skin tingle and her energy build. In the beginning she had to fight back the memory of that first day in the lake in order to concentrate but she learned to do so and in that way developed a greater level of control over her own thoughts.

Sometimes she would be instructed to hold an image in her mind as she did this exercise. Often it was an image of fire. She would build that fire from a small spark to a great flame. She could make that flame fill her entire mind and then her entire being. There were times when it felt as if she could make that blazing fire burn the world and those moments frightened and excited her in equal measure.

At other times she was told to run through a series of physical exercises that made the affects of this fire breathing on her body even more dramatic. She first moved her arms in sharp, fast circles around her head and then swung her legs forward and back in the same aggressive manner.

Then she would hunker on the ground with her hands and feet beneath her and hop something like a frog. Next, she lay on her back and curled herself upright into a sitting position.

She finished by standing up very tall and spreading her arms to the sky.

This combination of breathing and movement made her feel strong and focused. She didn't enjoy the unpleasant feelings she had to endure to get to his state but she liked this last feeling very much. She felt powerful.

The Crocodile often stressed to Ellie that there was a big difference between this state of body and mind and a state of panic. The Crocodile would lead Ellie silently out in the early morning and find a small group of deer, grazing calming together. The Crocodile would begin to make a deep, threatening noise from her belly and the mood of the deer would instantly change, the deer would lift their heads, their ears shooting up, their large eyes growing even wider.

"Watch closely," Ellie was instructed, "Watch their guts move fast but shallow. Watch the pulsing of the blood vessels in their necks, watch these animals become panicked. Learn to see the signs."

The Crocodile could stay hidden as long as she liked. She could slow her own breathing down so that she barely showed signs of life and yet still speak to Ellie in quiet, measured tones that seemed to bubble up from the earth itself.

She could slowly turn up the volume on the grunts and growls she was producing until the deer were completely out of their minds and fled blindly, rushing off in all directions from a threat they could not see or understand.

"You see," she would explain with great seriousness, "I can reach inside their bodies and manipulate them through their nerves, through their hormones, through their blood. I can control them and make them act as I want. When they scatter like that they are not in control. That is the last desperate hope of an animal totally consumed by fear. They simply flee and hope the one who falls, the one who is brought down by claws and teeth, is not them."

The Crocodile turned her head slowly so that one yellow eye was levelled steadily on Ellie, taking her all in with a single bite of her mind and said-

"Never allow yourself to be prey."

She stated it as a cold fact. Ellie understood that no response was asked for or expected.

As time passed Ellie became a little less frightened of the Crocodile but she was always left conflicted after their sessions. She loved, yes loved, the feeling of power, the Crocodile developed in her, but she feared the cruelty and ruthlessness she felt as she learned to chase down and destroy any trace of weakness, any trace of prey, left hiding within her.

Chapter 10

A note on names:

Names are important. The way that we understand the world and our place in it starts with names. The process of naming happens early when a child learns to speak its native language. Later the child doesn't remember doing it.

When we learn a new language we are naturally drawn towards learning a long list of nouns, the name words, even though verbs, the action words, might really be more useful. At the beginning of most books the writer starts with a long list of names. 'Who are the characters?' we ask as readers. 'Who is this story about?'

When we learn a new subject. Biology, Botany, Chemistry, Geography…, we start with a list of names: the names of body parts, the names of plants, the names of the elements, the names of countries or the features of the landscape.

In music, notes are names, we name the weather, we name our pets and our cuddly toys. We name our imaginary friends, we name our fears, we give names to the things that cause us pain.

We name colours, we name feelings and although most things are too complex to fit this name or that name (when does the colour red become the colour orange, where exactly is the dividing line) we suffer from a naming obsession.

Names are important.

Now Ellie wondered if she had a name. She wondered, if she had no name, did she have no value. She did not feel valueless, she did not feel uncared for. She did not, in fact, feel unloved.

But none of her teachers called her by any name.

And Ellie knew that she had a name. She couldn't quite remember it. There was just a sound, soft and difficult to capture. On evenings when she was alone she would ever so rarely play with the idea as she watched strange figures, like herself in shape and form, flicker in the shadows thrown by the fire that warmed her onto the wall of the cave that was her home and her prison.

And at the centre of that drama of shadows was an event she could not understand; could not even approach.

But she felt it would be wrong to ask her name, that it would break some sort of code.

Instead Ellie asked the Hare his name. She asked the Ape his name. She asked all of her teachers as it was natural for her to do and all of them gave her the same reply.

"I am not one thing; not one thing that can be named."

Then the Ape might say- "Come on child, we shall name all the plants that are good to eat and all the ones that are bad. That will be enough names for you today."

Then Ellie would spend some hours learning the names of plants you could eat, should eat, might eat in a pinch and definitely should never eat. She would learn their names in more than one language. She would learn Latin names and Common names. She learned that the same thing can have many different names. She came to understand that names are important and she learned that those same names can be slippery and untrustworthy.

Chapter 11

It was early morning. The Ape was showing Ellie how to identify a poisonous plant and beginning to teach her how to process it so as to extract that poison for use against an enemy in a manner that would be safe for her.

The plant was growing in that special part of the garden which housed examples of all the most dangerous poisonous plants in the world, a potentially deadly teaching tool for Ellie to understand the uses, abuses, properties and characteristics of these plants.

This one had drooping, violet flowers with a pale, whitish centre. It grew low to the earth and was not a very impressive thing to see.

"This plant is called Aconitum," the Ape explained, "It has many other names. It is called Wolfsbane and Leopardsbane and many other things in many languages. They call it after whatever frightens them the most, whatever animal makes them feel powerless. It doesn't normally grow well this far south but it is here for you to learn about and understand. In this garden we can reproduce whatever conditions we need to in order to educate you on the darker aspects of our friends the plants."

Ellie quickly surveyed the garden. It was full of variety, colour and beauty.

As if he could read her thoughts and feelings the Ape, with slightly raised voice, continued-

"Remember- this part of the garden is hell, this garden is death. These things grow here so that you can keep yourself safe from them and use them to keep those who might someday threaten you in danger FROM you. Attention now! This, this Aconitum you will find mostly in the mountains. It is not even to be touched by the ungloved hand. Its poison can pass through the skin and move to your heart. With the proper knowledge you can process it into a fine weapon. It has been strong enough to kill great whales when a spear's tip has been covered in it. After it is has done its work it is very hard to detect that it was ever present. With the correct understanding, with knowledge, it is potent indeed."

The Ape reached out with one finger and touched Ellie gently on the forehead.

"Always respect the power of these plants little one," he said, "or you will feel your stomach eating itself."

Ellie began to feel her stomach twist and cramp.

"Your skin will burn."

Ellie felt her face tingle and then prickle and then begin to burn as she felt a horrid pressure in her head and sweat begin to break out all over her body.

"Then your breathing will not obey you."

Indeed, she could feel your breath speeding up, her lungs struggling to take in air, a sharp pain came into her chest.

She tried to push the Ape's finger away but he held it there a few seconds longer.

"Remember.."

At that very moment The Hyena came bounding out of the trees, the Ape relinquished his control over Ellie and she collapsed to the ground. As she struggled to recover the Hyena approached her and thrust her wet nose and smelly jaws right into Ellie's own.

Ellie's first impression of the Hyena, as she refocused and took in the beast with her gaze, was dominated by two contrasting physical characteristics-

Two giant sad, gentle, brown eyes and one massive, powerful set of jaws. You might describe those jaws as 'bone-crushing' but that would not do them justice. Just looking at them you felt that they could crush anything and everything. They looked like they could crush things that were not even made of flesh and bone or other material things. They were soul-crushing jaws, if such a thing can be said to exist.

The Hyena pulled in a deep breath that seemed to Ellie to carry with it the entire chemical history of her short life in one action. Then the Hyena gently nudged the child in the chest and spoke-

"You have had a hard lesson this morning I can see and I can smell. Jump on my back and let's go for a run eh?"

Ellie was shocked. Her teachers were never this informal with her. The Hare was kind and the Ape had obviously softened to her in some ways, even if the Crocodile was as cold and unimpressed as she had been on the very first day they met, but none of them spoke to her this way. She was also understandably suspicious of what could happen when you let yourself be carried on someone's back.

"Jump on, we'll run, the air will clear your head and stomach of that terrible Hyena's Bane."

Oh well, there was nothing for it. Ellie climbed up as she was told and prepared for whatever might come.

As promised, it did clear her head. Riding on the Hyena's back was difficult at first. She was not shaped in a way that made her an easy vehicle. Her front end was so much larger than her rear that Ellie constantly felt she was going to slide off the back. That would have been a very bad thing too as the Hyena built up speed quickly and in only a few seconds she was moving too fast to safely get off, or fall off.

Still by this time Ellie was already a formidable character herself. She was strong far beyond her age. She found her spot and squeezed her legs together and fixed herself safely to the Hyena's fore shoulders. At first she held onto the dark mane for balance and stability but soon she was confidently riding with her hands free. She worried that she may be squeezing too hard for the Hyena's comfort so she asked.

"Ha," the Hyena laughed, "Squeeze away small one. It feels pleasant. If you would like, you can scratch my shoulders a little with those free hands. Put them to good use why not?"

Ellie did. The whole of the Hyena's back shivered with pleasure. Her fur was short and thick, spikey in many places and it felt good to dig her fingers deep in there and give the skin a good scratch.

They ran for miles, the Hyena displaying what seemed like a supernatural ability to maintain a path through the thickly packed trees. She perpetually appeared to be on the verge of ramming into a stocky trunk, turning smoothly a moment after it seemed too late to change course.

"Can you remember the path we are taking, little girl?" the Hyena called back without turning her head. "Can you map it in your mind?"

"No," Ellie shouted in honest reply, "No, I can't. You are running too fast."

"Your mind can be faster than I can run if you relax and let it do its work, remember that, practise that."

From that day on, several times a week. Ellie and the Hyena practised the skills necessary to navigate in the wild. When she was ready the Hyena would take Ellie deep into the forest on her back and then abandon her.

"Find your way home."

Was all she would say and then disappear.

The first time Ellie spent three days finding her way back.

On her first night alone she found a soft mound of earth that she thought would be perfect to lie down on to sleep. She lay down to rest her aching limbs. She looked at the tiny part of the sky she could spy through the canopy of the forest and began to relax.

Then she felt something lightly touching the skin on her arm. She bushed her arm absent-mindedly with a single finger.

As she settled back down she felt a similar feeling on her left leg, then her right leg, both arms, now her shoulders…

She jumped up when she felt the first bite. Like a small, extremely sharp needle piercing her skin. Then all at once there was biting all over her body. Once she saw the first ant she realised there were ants all over her. They had large pinchers on their heads and they were digging them into her flesh. She grabbed an ant and pulled it off. The head stayed stuck to her arm as the body came away. They were fierce and strong, willing to die to keep hold of their grip.

She realised that she could never pull each of these little beasts off her one by one. She'd be eaten alive first.

An idea came to her instinctively. She ran, looking for water and all the time the ants bit and bit.

It was twenty-five agonizing minutes until she found a very small muddy pool. She pulled her simple, woven clothes off and leapt in. She rolled around in the shallow water until the biting stopped. She remained in the water far longer than she probably needed to in order to make sure that all the ants were definitely gone.

Her skin was still burning and tingling as she left the pool and collapsed on the bank. Somehow, after how long she would never know, and despite the way her flesh still burned she fell into a deep sleep.

The next morning she woke still stinging and in pain and realised that she was completely lost.

She had no idea where she had taken herself in her search for the pool. She had to abandon the mental map she had drawn in her head while the Hyena had taken her deep into the forest and she could not be more totally and hopelessly lost. She started that second day cold and hungry. She had soon given up on trying to find and remove all the ant heads from her body and every part of her was sore.

She wished that the Hyena would come and take her home. She could imagine the Hyena carefully grooming her,

picking off the heads of the soldier ants with a
gentleness that belied the brutal strength of her jaws.

She did not allow herself that silly hope for long.
That hope would not help; it would only make her weak.
The Crocodile would be disappointed in her.

She understood that panic was not her friend. The heart
of her training in any situation was calm composure. She
must always remain calm and clear thinking.

What was her situation? What could she do to improve
it?

She tried to remember where she had run when she fled
her camp. She shut her eyes and concentrated hard. It was
no use. There was only a confusion of trees and shades of
light and dark to be found in her memory.

What else could she do?

Her tracks. She would have left tracks in the leaves as
she ran with heavy step. If she could find them she could
get back to the place she had tried to sleep the previous
night and from there could trace the path she had
memorised from the high and speedy vantage point of the

Hyena's back. She wished she were on that back now but forced that thought aside again and concentrated on finding those tracks.

She walked slowly around the edge of the pool scrutinizing the earth. If she had been worried about finding tracks she was wrong, there were too many of them.

She found the marks of deer, birds, and of larger animals that left the clear impression of impressive and dangerous claws. She persisted, however, and with patience and a keen eye she found her own. She was struck by how distinctive they were; different from all the rest somehow. Perhaps it was simply because they were her own but it felt like something more. She sometimes encountered this feeling, a sense of being somehow out of place in a profound way, prompted by small things like this or the sight and feel of her clothes, simple though they were, fashioned from the same woven hemp that was used to create the door to her alcove in the caves, as she put them on in the morning.

Again, she fought this distraction. The Ape was constantly warning her of the dangers that flowed from how easily and how often her mind wandered.

He told her over and over to do one thing, and one thing only, at a time. He reminded her that one thing should not become two but Ellie's mind seemed to her to naturally split and skip and travel in many directions in much the same way that the many and varied tracks left this pool and moved off into the forest along such a great number of individual paths. It was a constant battle for her, to control her own busy mind.

She followed her own tracks. With great concentration she was able to see the frantic path she had cut through the trees.

Her movement had not always made sense, had not always followed the most direct line but then she had not known where she was headed and had not been exactly thinking straight. She imagined herself running wildly like a deer being harassed by a fly and she smiled, she must have made a funny sight for whichever animals were around to see her fleeing from what must have appeared to be an invisible enemy.

Then she realised that she would also have made a very obvious target if anything large with teeth, claws and the big, hungry, forward facing eyes of a night time hunter had been around to watch. She remembered the words of the Crocodile, spoken in her soft but intense tone of voice-

"Do not allow yourself to be prey."

She shivered.

Her progress was steady but slow. A journey that could have been measured in minutes at a run now was slowly eked out in hours. At last, though, she found herself back at the place she had been seeking, looking down at the large anthill she had tried to make her pillow.

She spent a little time watching the ants. She was not inclined to have friendly feelings towards them but she did admire their busy industry and the fierce self-assurance they displayed. She did not; however, want to give them any cause to attack her again, so she moved on immediately, back on the path the Hyena had taken at last.

She was hungry now and she gathered some fungi and plants she knew to be healthy and nutritious, if not terribly satisfying. She was grateful to the Ape for all the hours and days of instruction in what to eat and what to avoid. She was grateful to the Hyena too as she was finding that she could follow the mind-map she had created of the journey back home with something like confidence now.

That evening she was grateful to the Hare who had shown her long ago how to make a good fire and how to bring vegetation together to make a comfortable bed; why had she not remembered this and put it to use before making a bed of an ant-hill she wondered now. The whole incident was at least starting to feel a little funny.

She was even grateful to the Crocodile, who alone among her teachers still seemed to regard her as no more than an annoyance and was constantly cold and dismissive with her, who had taught her how to use her deep breathing to bring her mind and body to rest when it came time to sleep.

An hour or so from home the next day it started to rain. To call it hard rain would be to describe it with too little force. This was the sort of rain that doesn't so much fall as fill the space between earth and sky entirely so that you feel you are walking under water. Still she knew she was nearly home. The timing was good. She had almost beaten the rain to her destination.

It was nearing the end of the third day when Ellie arrived back at the mouth of her cave. She was tired, soaking wet and still hungry but she felt as if she had proved something. She felt quite grown up and independent. She felt quite proud.

"Oh, child," the Hyena's voice was sad as she appeared from the direction of the trees and began to lick Ellie with her rough tongue, "You will need to do better when it comes time for the test."

Now Ellie looked at herself in a new light. She saw that she was soaked to the skin, filthy, her clothes were torn, she was covered from top to toe in ant bites and, yes, the Hyena had already picked two leeches from her that she had not even noticed were there, enjoying a meal of her blood. She realised that it had taken her three days to do something she should have done in less than one. All her confidence disappeared and left her feeling like a helpless child.

The Hyena saw the look of disappointment on Ellie's face.

"You don't give up, though, do you," she consoled in a honey-sweet tone, "You persist and you endure and with that you can develop all the other things you need. If you are given time."

Ellie suddenly felt very tired. She hugged the Hyena, stretching her arms as far as she could around her hairy neck and did something she seldom did.

She cried.

She cried deep and for a long time and the Hyena stood watch over her crying and said nothing. When all the tears were out of her Ellie stood up as straight as she could to face the Hyena, wiped her eyes as best she could, and said-

"I can improve."

The Hyena sort of purred and growled together in a strange cat/dog tone she sometimes made.

As Ellie turned to enter the cave for much needed proper rest a question lit up in her mind, sudden and strong.

"What is 'The Test'?" she asked, turning back to the Hyena.

The Hyena almost blushed, if such a thing were possible.

"I talk too much little one," she said, "you should sleep now."

She hesitated and then added, in a quick, breathless voice-

"But remember I will always protect and help you if I can."

Then the Hyena turned and bounded off.

In the days that followed Ellie thought about 'The Test' the Hyena had accidently mentioned.

She had had tests before. Often. The Ape was particularly fond of testing her on any and every subject under the sun. With warning, without warning, the Ape was one who believed in the value of tests. This; however, was THE test, that single world was the one that had caused Ellie to pay special attention.

That word and something in the expression on the Hyena's face and in her tone of voice when she referred to it.

**THE TEST**.

The Hyena would say no more about it though, no matter how often she asked.

Eventually the Hyena became uncharacteristically aggressive, snapping her jaws together in a terrifying gesture that told Ellie the subject was closed.

Chapter 12

<u>A note on death</u>:

After the horrible first day with the Crocodile in the lake Ellie began to pay more attention to death.

All being well a young child will usually have only vague ideas about death and have no experience with it directly.

Ellie was unusual in that death had been all around her since she first came to this place. She saw one animal kill another animal to eat. She saw this everyday. She witnessed the struggles between predator and prey. She saw animals kill and she saw them die. She saw animals eat other animals alive. She saw a never-ending battle to keep young ones safe and also fed.

She saw plants die too and she watched them decay forming, as she learned from the Ape, new soil that fed new, young, strong trees and grass.

She had not been shielded from death and so she saw it as part of a natural cycle; as part of a transition or as a by-product of the need for food or, observing some of the animals, the need for dominance.

That last thing, violent death arising from the need for dominance was the only one she found disturbing. The more intelligent and social animals were the ones most inclined to fight for dominance, even to bully those weaker than themselves to reinforce their own higher rank but it was always a shock to see an animal go so far as to kill another for top position, to go that far after victory had already been achieved. It seemed unnecessary and wasteful and Ellie had no taste for it.

Even with death so close to her, Ellie had not felt it as a personal threat  before the Crocodile nearly drowned her. She had never conceived of it, the way writers do, as a grim figure, a hunter to be feared, an evil to be avoided.

Now she thought she should probably pay more attention to it as a thing in itself, an end that could come without warning and without reason to HER. The fact that it could come without reason disturbed her greatly.

She thought about it at night. She saw so many possible ways that she could meet her end in the shadows the fire threw on the cave wall. She knew the large beasts that could kill her with their strength and speed. She was aware of the small animals that could kill with poison and venom, bites and stings. There were plants that could kill also. She might fall from a tree. Any of the giant beasts that were her guardians and educators could kill her on a whim.

Death became a more personal presence in her mind. Death became a monster and it brought fear with it.

It was the Hare who noticed that Ellie was different in the days after the Crocodile's arrival. He saw it in the way she moved. She was more timid and less joyful in how she ran, jumped, climbed and swam. She looked around more, seemed more watchful, but became, in fact, less observant. She was showing all the signs of anxiety.

So, one evening the Hare sat with Ellie in front of the fire and asked-

"What is wrong child?"

At first Ellie avoided the question but the Hare was persistent and before too long Ellie admitted that she had become afraid to die. She was worried. She was embarrassed to admit her weakness.

The Hare did not mock her or tell her to be strong. He thought seriously for a moment and then said-

"Think of the way that you have been shown how to make medicines. Do you not find the plants for these medicines in the same garden as the ones you use to make poisons?"

It was true, Ellie had learned how to make liniments for bruises and poultices for broken bones from plants that could both kill and cure. Of all the plants that lived in the same garden some were deadly and others were healthful. Indeed, some of the plants used for healing could also be used to harm if they were processed and mixed in a different manner. A small amount of a plant that caused vomiting could be used to purge yourself of a different poison. There was a constant, complex and intricate interplay between the useful and what was to be feared.

"What is the difference between the safe and the unsafe plants?"

The Hare asked.

Ellie thought hard. There was no easy answer. There was no one colour that meant danger. No simple code. She had studied long and with great effort to learn what was good and what was bad. Then it hit her.

"Knowledge," she replied.

"Yes," the Hare smiled. "There is no cure for danger in the world. Nothing can make it disappear. But knowledge, as you have yourself identified, and practice, these are the things that mean you can live safely no matter what you face and sometimes even joyfully."

The Hare patted her on the head.

The Hare left and Ellie settled back on her bedding. If Death was a hunter, she thought, she was already making herself a very hard target, one no sensible predator would choose.

Chapter 13

After years of living in the hard wild and training with the great animal creatures we have been calling the Hare, the Ape, the Crocodile and the Hyena, Ellie was comfortable with the presence and in the close company of massive, intimidating beasts. She was used to being close to this hybrid species of animal and mythical monster.

She took for granted a world that was alien to its core and ran counter to logic. She was almost entirely, if not quite completely, a native in a very strange land indeed.

That did not stop her being impressed by the Wolf when he arrived. He was the largest of all the monstrous, beautiful beasts and the most intimidating.

He was grey and black and brown and white all interwoven; separating and combining in patterns Ellie would find fascinating to watch from that moment on and for as long as she knew him.

His paws were so large that they left tracks in soft earth so broad and so deep that Ellie could hop into them with both feet and sink to way above her ankles. His tracks could fill to become small pools after rain. His size and power could alter the landscape he moved through but if he chose he could pass through the forest without leaving so much as a mark on the carpet of leaves that made up a whole world for the insects, rodents, lizards and other small creatures which it sustained.

With soft thread or hard he could run tirelessly for endless hours at a swift pace that silently told all that here was the master of the land. His stride chewed up miles and he seemed to know the landscape, to own it, more than merely pass through it.

As he approached Ellie for the first time she stood her ground. Long ago she had been taught that-

"If you were going to run you should already be gone; if not be confident and stand."

The Hare had taught her this and the slight twitch of his whiskers as he spoke the words had told her that he had learned the lesson himself and through some sort of bitter experience which he kept private.

This mantra combined in her mind with the dictate of the Crocodile-

"Never be prey."

Before any creature, however large and fierce, before Death itself if need be, and if ever there was a convincing picture of Death the teeth of the Wolf certainly qualified, she could not and would not appear weak.

The Wolf approached her slowly, lowering his head and licking the air between them just once. He seemed to be making an effort not too show his enormous teeth which Ellie understood as a kindness. This understanding helped her to relax a little. He continued towards her slowly, as unthreatening as it was possible for him to be.

When she was fairly sure that he was not about to snap her in two and enjoy her as a snack Ellie relaxed enough to take a good long look at him.

The Wolf was a picture of tightly controlled force and fury. The physical form he occupied seemed barely able to contain him. Even in rest his muscles constantly rippled as if a gentle stream of energy was working under the skin, feeding every inch of him. When he was calm he was like a mountain at rest and when, as she would see later, he exploded he was like nature itself, more comparable to a storm than to an animal.

Then the Wolf turned and walked slowly away. He said nothing and left Ellie to a normal day.

Chapter 14

For weeks the Wolf just watched Ellie. He did not speak.

He followed Ellie when she was doing physical training with the Hare.

He watched when she fought the Ape and was turned inside out and rolled up in a ball but fought on, and fought on with as much intelligence as fury, forever looking for angles and opportunities for small advantage.

He watched her going through her breathing techniques with the Crocodile, who seemed extremely unhappy to be anywhere near the Wolf. They would not even greet one another but only cast suspicious glances between them.

He followed her as she ran through the forest after the Hyena, learning to navigate and trail-find.

His presence was constant and intimidating, like the thunder that carries the promise of an approaching storm.

Ellie often felt like she was being hunted. Worse perhaps, for when one is hunted you know exactly what the hunter wants.

In those first weeks she only heard the Wolf voice one sentence. After he had watched her go through a sparring session with the Ape she heard him say, under his breath and certainly to himself but clear enough, his voice being so huge-

"The old go to the teeth of the young."

One morning no one came to wake Ellie or bring breakfast. She waited for the Hare as she ran through her morning exercises but she remained alone.

Curious, she wandered outside and there she found the Wolf. Sitting tall as a tree and looking down on her as if he had been waiting.

For the first time he spoke directly to her-

"I will not wait on you child, in any sense."

Ellie was thinking of breakfast, just hungry enough not to be anxious about doing something wrong.

"Walk and listen."

Ellie followed behind the Wolf, without her beloved breakfast, feeling like a duckling following a buffalo.

Even when he was clearly walking slowly it was hard to keep up. She would find out just how hard it was to keep up with him as time passed and day after day he would walk relentlessly and make her follow, listening and repeating what he had to say for mile after mile and over and over again.

"Today you begin to learn how to manage yourself and the world. Listen. Ask no questions. I do not wish to have to discipline you because you are so small I fear I might break you, but I will, if need be. Sometimes things or people break and it is sad but that does not mean the reason they were broken was poor or unjust."

Ellie almost asked what he meant by that but stopped herself just in time.

"You have some brains clearly. Let us see if we can use them for more than soup."

Was that a sly smile?

The Wolf did not break his stride as he continued-

"Think honestly. Understand yourself, your strengths and weaknesses honestly."

He paused for a moment.

"Think honestly, it is more difficult than it at first appears. Just as the nervous system contrives to make damaged bodies function bypassing damaged muscles and finding any possible means of compensation, so the mind conceals weakness so that the image of a whole personality is preserved. You must learn to acknowledge the thoughts, feelings and instincts that threaten as well as nurture you. You must leave no weaknesses buried deep within you and undiscovered, waiting for an enemy to exploit and manipulate you with. Do not allow yourself to be led about on invisible strings that you know nothing about. If your weakness is not your own it will belong to others and they will own a part of you as powerful as your strengths. You must be ruthless in hunting down and killing the lies you will tell yourself."

They walked for some time in silence, Ellie trying to make sense of the words. Her brow furrowed like a ploughed field in concentration.

The Wolf observed this and seemed pleased.

"It is a practice and not a state. Have it always in your mind. Think honestly,…" and he repeated himself.

So the days passed. Ellie walked and listened and thought. The Wolf repeated the same formulae over and over.

"Learn about all the ways of the world and the ways of all animals, the better to understand your own way," he intoned. "Look with clear eyes, a hunter must possess clear eyes always, and see the ways of the world for what they truly are. Reflect on the interactions of all creatures with each other and with the world and bring that understanding to bear on your own behaviour. Learn to understand yourself. It is a practice."

"Understand the difference between winning and losing when it is important. You must understand that sometimes you must lose in order to learn and grow but at other times it is of primary importance that you win. Learn to recognise this difference if you are to live and thrive."

"Pay attention to the small things and see past the surface to learn what is real. See what is not being shown and what is being actually hidden, deliberately or otherwise. You must see through to honest intention in others. To trust in your own good judgment you must first develop good judgment. This is a practice."

"Do nothing that is useless. You do not have time. You have time enough to do all you need but not time for anything else. You must know what is useless and what is of use and make your life useful. This is a practice."

At first Ellie only listened. Later the Wolf made her repeat this code over and over. Later still he questioned her on her understanding of what he was teaching.

He drilled her and drilled her in these rules. He made her repeat them time without number. He required that she get every word right. She was allowed no leeway. She could not rephrase anything her own way. She learned them by rote and perfectly.

The Wolf held separate lessons on how to deal with Human Beings specifically. Human Beings got their own treatment, he explained, as they were remarkably difficult and they would make up a large part of her work when the time came."

He still refused to give Ellie a clear description of what that work might be. He would only make it clear that it would be hard and demanding and that failure would surely cost her her life.

He instructed her to think about humans in three ways.

1-Ways in which they are just like other animals.

2-Ways in which they are basically the same but sometimes do something different or confusing.

3-Ways in which they are unique, and uniquely troubling.

This study went on day after day. The Wolf was relentless. He did not notice when Ellie was becoming bored and tired; then very bored indeed and exhausted. Everything about him suggested that if he had noticed, he would not have cared even the slightest bit.

So when the morning came that he informed Ellie that they were going on a journey she was both relieved and happy. She asked no questions about where they were going or what their purpose was.

"You may climb to my back," said the Wolf, "We have many miles to travel and we must go quickly."

The Wolf lowered himself as he spoke, turning his head slightly to indicate that Ellie should mount his shoulders.

It was something of a climb to get there. Once in place below his neck Ellie did not feel the pleasant sense of comfort and fun that she always had when she was carried by the Hyena. The Wolf's shoulders were far too broad and she was sure that playfully scratching his fur was quite out of the question.

The Wolf took off at a frightening speed. Ellie, not for the first time, wished she were bigger and stronger than she was. She clung with all her might and tried, as the Hyena had conditioned her to do, to scan and memorize the landscape through which they rushed.

They left the borders of the forest and passed the lake. Beyond the lake there was flat, empty grassland for miles, brown and dry grass punctuated only sparsely by little copses of weak looking trees. They tore through this as if the Devil was after them but then, the Devil would no doubt have found his match in the Wolf.

The Wolf never stopping, sure in his path and Ellie clinging on, looking from side to side where she could, learning what little she could about the land they were travelling through.

Next they came to some small, rolling hills, framed by mountains in the background and the first human settlement Ellie had seen in years. Farms, little family farms divided up the land before the villages began, popping up like anthills as Ellie's gaze travelled towards the mountains.

Ellie felt suddenly sick. She felt dizzy and only stopped herself fainting and falling from the Wolf's back with some emergency breathing.

The Wolf stopped. Just far enough away from the cows and pigs not to be seen.

Ellie did not want to be here. Something was frightening her more than she could remember since the Crocodile had made her feel what being next to death was like.

She wanted to go home to her cave. She wished to go home now. Her fear was so great that she almost voiced it to the Wolf but she knew, deep down, even in her near panic, that it would do no good. She registered this out of proportion fear as a weakness to be examined, though she was not at all sure if she could look deep into it without falling and falling, possibly too far to recover, possibly forever.

She had to go on with an unsettling combination of submission and persistence.

They crouched down behind a mound of earth and grass and the Wolf addressed the girl-

"What did I teach you about humans?"

Ellie repeated what she had learned by heart. The words flowed out of Ellie, quick and automatic. She could almost see them leave her mouth like bees streaming out of a hive.

"We think about humans in three ways. 1-Ways in which they are just like other animals. 2-Ways in which they are basically the same but sometimes do something different or confusing. 3-Ways in which they are unique, and uniquely troubling."

"Watch now," said the Wolf, "See there, that child playing, stamping about and making noise with his childish songs. He approaches now the home of a poisonous snake. Watch and see."

Ellie looked as the child played. She felt torn between simply watching as the Wolf told her and doing something to warn this little boy. She felt a strange sensation of responsibility towards him, small and weak as he seemed, as he made his blind way towards the place where the snake made its home.

Why would she feel any more sympathy for this boy than for any other animal that might disturb a resting snake? There was no time to consider this question now.

With horrible inevitability the child brought a clumsy foot down on the snake's nest. The snake rose up angry and ready to fight but thankfully did not immediately strike. The boy screamed in fright and ran as fast as he could, already shaking furiously with fear.

"You see," said the Wolf, "just like any other small prey animal. He flees in blind terror. He is no different to the deer in the forest when they see the wolf leap from the bushes."

Next the Wolf brought her close to the edge of a village.

"From here you go alone. There is a hut just there ahead and you will approach it without being seen. If you are seen find your own way back to your cave unpursued or do not come back. In the hut you will be able to see two old man sitting on opposite sides of a table. Observe what they do. Come back to me here. Go."

Ellie crouched low and moved swiftly and silently towards the small group of huts at the very edge of the village. It was good to be moving, doing as the Hyena taught her in her own forest. She passed a low wooden fence behind which three large black pigs grunted and rattled and she barely disturbed them. She was not there; not available to be seen or felt or smelt on the air. She was invisible. This was a feeling she loved.

Through the large window of the nearest dwelling she saw the two old men. Toothless, and leathery skinned they sat in silence at opposite sides of a small table on which was placed a board. The board was divided into light and dark squares and on some of these squares Ellie saw black or white pebbles placed. The two men sat staring hard at the board, as if the pebbles might suddenly spring into some sort of action.

Instead, after what seemed a very long interval, one of the men lifted a bony hand and moved one of the black pebbles to a different square.

Then more waiting.

Ellie wondered why the Wolf had sent her here. She stared hard looking for the lesson and, with the passing of minutes and much concentration, she saw it. She noticed the way the men were breathing. She saw the blood vessels in the neck of the man who was yet to move a pebble throbbing as if he were running from a predator. She noticed the narrowed pupils of their eyes and she realised that they were both hugely physically stressed.

Something about this board and these pebbles was causing them to react as if they were fighting for their lives.

"Sometimes they act like other animals but with strange differences." Ellie thought and she returned to the Wolf to tell him so.

The Wolf merely nodded.

"Come with me."

They walked in silence until they were out of sight of the village and then the Wolf ordered Ellie up on his shoulders.

She climbed up and almost before she was ready he was off towards the mountains.

The ground rose steeply and more steeply still as they encountered the first mountainous slopes. There were no more fields. Narrow tracks became no tracks at all and still the Wolf relentlessly climbed, his pace never slackening, the air growing colder and thinner around them.

They came to a cave. A small, dirty grey thing unlike Ellie's home. There was no comfort here and no warmth. It was a place to be fled from, not returned to.

The Wolf stopped and Ellie jumped down from his back. They walked inside slowly and in silence. The Wolf sniffed the stale air; Ellie could sense his disgust and she shared it. There was something deeply wrong in this empty place. "Leave it empty," something inside her said, "Leave it empty, just leave."

A bad memory was living here, sucking in all the clean air and breathing out pollution.

The Wolf walked to a corner at the back and began to dig. It only took him a few sweeps with one paw to uncover a shallow hole in which there were some white objects in a small pile.

The Wolf called Ellie to him and directed her to look. She saw some bones. The Wolf touched one of the longer ones lightly.

"Pick up the bone and hold it."

Ellie did not want to but she did what she was told; even if she did so slowly.

"Now close your eyes and listen to my words."

"This is the femur of a girl about your age. It is the largest bone from the leg."

Ellie concentrated on the Wolf's voice and as she did a picture appeared in her mind. It was a clear, sharp picture, no shake, no softness at the edges.

She saw a girl of about her own age. A thin girl with haunted eyes and sharp cheekbones. The look she wore was similar to one Ellie had observed fall upon the faces of aging or sick animals before they removed themselves from their social groups to die. The girl was a living ghost.

"This girl had no name," the Wolf continued, "It is not that I don't know her name or that her name has been forgotten. She was not given the basic honour of a name. She was not given a name because it was felt that she had no value. She was a third daughter so it was nothing unusual for her family to feel that way. They were not unusual or unfeeling. They were normal, decent members of their community. This girl was a burden too far on the family resources. Well, she would have been. It was decided that she should be abandoned. She was given to her uncle, her father's younger brother because he was the first to agree to do it. He was to bring her here to the mountains and leave her. Nature then would take its course, as they like to say when they cannot be honest about the things that they do themselves. They might have questioned why this uncle was so willing to do something others found so unpleasant but if the work was to be done, who wanted to second guess the one willing to take it on?"

The picture grew in intensity within the confines of Ellie's mind. The girl being taken away by her uncle, not fighting or screaming but doing as she was told. A girl used to doing as she was told, aware that it was the only course of action that would be tolerated from her.

"I said that the child had no value but unfortunately she had some value to this uncle. She could do two things this uncle valued. She could sew as she had small precise hands and sharp eyesight, and she could suffer."

The Wolf's voice faltered a little, just a little; and a shiver ran under his fur that jumped across the cold space between them and transferred to Ellie's flesh, running up her back and burrowing in like a tic.

"This man liked fine things and liked his clothes to have fine, intricate stitching, and he liked to see suffering. Here was his chance to have a supply of both just for himself. So he did not let her die. He kept her here as his slave. He beat her and for no other reason than he liked to beat her. He kept her almost starved all the time. When she was not working he chained her up there."

The Wolf indicated two holes in the wall of the cave and Ellie saw the chains that had once been bolted in there lying on the ground.

"But after a time she was too weak to even try to escape. The chains were not necessary. He made her stitch beautiful flowers and animals into his clothes and he told no one but deep down in his heart he felt that the suffering of the girl made the clothes more beautiful."

They stood in silence for some time. Ellie did not look at the Wolf. She was looking at the little girl from long ago, trying to find some hope in that face but finding none. She felt tears begin to collect in her eyes. She squeezed them tightly shut and tried to find in this story something other than horror. There was nothing else.

"Sometimes it is impossible to understand why they do what they do," she said to the Wolf.

They left the cave and travelled home in silence.

Chapter 15

Ellie's life was dominated by routine and she had grown into a creature of habit. Her day-to-day existence was controlled as surely by a strict routine as it was run by the Ape, the Hare or any of her other, strict mentors.

This constant structure nurtured her and gave her the strength to get through the hardest days of training without complaining or giving up. The lack of choice meant that she found it easier to repeatedly do the challenging and strenuous things she had to do. It allowed her to be persistent and being a small animal in a tough world, persistence was her best lifeline.

The Ape had once told her-

"Discipline is your ally; discipline is the foundation on which everything else is built."

She grew steadily into understanding that maxim with her years of training.

She woke before the full dawn of every new day, the most adventurous fingers of first light just reaching into her sleeping quarters and nudging her gently awake.

She ate the same simple, nutritious food. It was important that she thought of food as fuel and not pleasure or entertainment. She had to stay strong and lean and could not afford to expend thought or emotion on preferences for tastes or types of food.

In truth, however, she harboured a great love for the sweetness of honey. She would hunt it out for herself when she could, at some risk from angry bees. Other times the Hare would bring her some honey; handing it to her with pleasure and advising her to eat it quickly and not mention it to the Ape or the Wolf.

She ran through the same set of physical and breathing exercises to make her ready for the work of the day. That was the time when she felt she became herself, inhabited her body and took her place in the world.

The content of the day's study was all that varied, depending on which teacher she was working with and which subject they were concentrating on at that time. The intensity and seriousness never varied.

Her training went in cycles; sometimes placing more emphasis on fighting or instead, sometimes on wilderness survival, or any of the other essential elements of her education, so that she had an opportunity to recover mentally and physically from the specific demands of each discipline.

She spent her time with a small, closed group of intense and demanding instructors who allowed her very little softness; although the Hare and the Hyena found it harder and harder as time passed to hide the warmth they felt for the brave and resourceful little human being. The Hare fretted over any injury and the Hyena had the anxious air of a mother when she lectured Ellie about the dangers of the weather, how it could kill her quicker than any animal on stormy nights.

Every evening, unless she was out tracking and camping with the Hyena, she slept again in the same small, cosy alcove in her part of the cave.

She meditated and stored the lessons of the day inside her; then slept a mostly dreamless sleep to recover and be ready for the following day.

Dreams, when they did come, broke her routine for they were anxious and alien and left her feeling uncomfortable and unrested. On the mornings that followed nights that she did suffer the arrival of dreams, however, her routine was there to greet her and restore her to herself.

In this way she was shaped by her constant practice and became perfectly suited to it.

If she were to have been lifted up and placed in a different environment she would have been a very strange child indeed. Her training had taught her to be extremely relaxed when the opportunity to do so was presented and violently alert and active when action was called for.

She would have been a frightening, anti-social child in any schoolyard- the kind a young teacher would be fascinated with and ultimately frustrated by within a school year. But for the demands that her present life placed upon her she was becoming perfectly suited.

Now and then, as the time passed, the Wolf briefly reminded her that there would be a test. He would answer no questions about it but the fact of the test was no longer hidden. He used it as motivation. If her resolve was flagging in training or her study lacked some intensity he might tell her that she should improve her effort as the test would come some day. He would say it very seldom and gave her no details. He said it just often enough to never let it quite fade from her mind.

Chapter 16

When she awoke one morning in a different place to the one where she had gone to sleep the night before she immediately understood that something very serious was happening.

She had a cloudy memory of something similar happening many years ago and, combined with the break in her routine, she felt immediately and seriously threatened.

The atmosphere had been more tense than usual, more urgent around her of late. Perhaps she should have realised something big was coming. For now she must take stock of her surroundings, see what was possible and decide what was best to do.

She was underground. The place was not unlike her cave in some ways but it smelled damp and dirty and the only traces of light were leaking in from above her, not from any obvious entrance.

She knew instinctively that the Hare was not coming with food. She felt, in her stomach, that this was going to be a dreadful day.

**The Test.**

It could only be that the time had come for the test the Wolf had spoken of and the existence of which the Hyena had let slip long before.

She was frozen briefly. She was not fearful for her safety, she was frozen rather by the seriousness of the moment.

She understood that her life had been building to this point. All the work and the pain and sacrifice, all the routine; fighting the strange, sad feeling she had sometimes at night watching those weird, shadowy figures on the cave wall.

Those figures came to her now strongly. Ghostly human figures both known and unknown. Known in her blood but unknown in her life. For a moment she was falling into dreams of a different life, one totally alien to her, an easier, softer life that she had to simply ignore because she instinctively understood that these visions were like the roots of plants that would grow strong and crack and break up the earth if allowed to develop. They would destroy her foundations. She gave them no oxygen.

Her job now was to get home and in order to get home she must first get out. She must get safely out of this place.

She took some quick, sharp breaths, inhaling longer than she exhaled, attempting to get the most energy she could from the thick and dirty air.

She let her eyes adjust to the darkness and began to see the outlines of the space she was in more clearly. The floor was uncovered dirt and there was nothing in the room with her except a set of wooden steps that led upwards to a closed wooden door, a trapdoor in the floor of a room above her head.

She climbed the stairs slowly making sure not to produce any creaks from the old and dusty wood. She was wary but she knew that she had the positional advantage on anyone coming down the steps. She reached up and tested the trapdoor in the ceiling. It moved. It was not locked and nothing was weighing it into place from above. In that sense at least she was not trapped.

She hesitated, focused, quieted her mind and listened to the room above. There were voices. They spoke quietly, almost in a whisper, but they were there.

Three male voices. They were on the other side of the room from where she would emerge as she came through the trapdoor. There was so much unknown to her. To enter that room now would put her at a great strategic disadvantage but she could not stay where she was, locked by fear into a musty cage.

It was the Devil's choice but one she had to make.

She opened the trap door just a little and managed a furtive look around the room.

There were the three men she had heard. They were sitting around a small table on short-legged stools. Otherwise the room was empty.

Ellie sized them up. Two middle-aged men, not so large or strong and a boy just leaving his teens. She saw no obvious weapons but she had so little time to take it all in. She lowered the door.

It was an uncertain situation. She didn't have enough time to plan, to make a strategy. She would not have chosen these terms of engagement but she could not stay hesitating where she was.

Maybe the men meant her no harm and would let her pass with no trouble. Maybe this was not even the test. In her gut she knew this was not true.

She remembered all the times that she had faced off with the Ape to spar. Sometimes she had been so exhausted that she could barely lift her own arms to defend herself. That dreadful feeling of total fatigue had made her want to quit but the Ape would never allow her to.

The time comes to act whether you want it to or you wish for it not to come with all your heart; and when the time comes you must respond. She had been taught that how she performed when she was at her worst and weakest had to be good enough to survive. Sometimes there was nothing for it but to rely on the violence of action to get you through. Yes, sometimes you needed to crash through uncertainty like a great wave.

She lifted the door and emerged. There was no other way to do it; no opportunity to have surprise and stealth on her side.

The first assault came from the light coming through the window hitting her hard in the eyes. It half blinded her. She could only dimly make out the hazy outline of the men turning their heads towards her.

She focused on the door and made straight for it. If she were allowed to leave untroubled then she would do so. She felt this day would be long and arduous and she would avoid any unnecessary struggle if she could.

She was not to be so lucky. The two older men stood. They did not come straight for her, instead they moved to block her path to the door boxing her in, as she had seen hunting animals do so often in her forest.

Fine, that was their choice and would be their fate; she would not be prey today.

They moved towards her from both sides. They tried to take hold of her but she was accustomed to much bigger and stronger hands gripping her and they had no hope of holding on.

Perhaps they underestimated her because of her size and age. If so, they didn't do so for long. She twisted swiftly and struck expertly. They were broken and bloody before their minds could catch up with what was happening. They were lost in the face of her skill and experience.

She turned to face the younger man. He looked at her with as much conviction as he could manage for a moment but he couldn't hold it. Ellie took one menacing step forward. He leapt through the window and ran.

She burst out the door still ready to fight, the resistance she had received thus far had barely warmed her up, and found herself in a normal little town. The street was quiet and peaceful. It was paved with a bright yellow clay that she had not seen before. There were two children playing happily not so far from where she stood.

There was absolutely nothing threatening to be seen anywhere around her. She searched her environment for any sign of danger- nothing.

It almost felt like a trap.

"Keep going," she thought, "Keep going while you can."

She decided on the shortest distance out of the town and set off walking; not too quickly but as fast as she felt she could without drawing attention to herself. She concentrated on being invisible, willing herself not to be noticed.

She passed one or two old people sitting outside their dwellings in the sun. She avoided eye contact, looking down slightly and using her peripheral vision, doing her best to control the raging tension inside her.

She reached the edge of the settlement quickly and without incident. She was not far from the edge of a forest, her territory. If she got there things would immediately be better for her.

She was beginning to relax a little when she heard a storm gathering behind her. She felt it like a threatening alteration in the weather, a change in the air. She willed it to pass, to be nothing to do with her, a mistake in her perception due to her fear and excitement.

It was only for a moment, a forlorn hope. She turned her head to see what she would face next...

...And saw the dogs. Where they came from and who released them she would never learn. There were five of them. Huge beasts; an uncertain mix of the larger local breeds. Their muzzles were scarred from years of fighting. Their muscles were carved as if from stone from years of contention, hard conditions and killing.

The tallest was brown with bald patches on his shoulders. He would have stood easily head and shoulders above a grown man if he rose on his hind legs.

There were two who must have been closely related. Shorter than the brown one but even broader and thicker than he. They were pure black and had short muzzles with jaws that looked like a mauling death.

The remaining two were shorter again but built like canine tanks. Every movement of their bodies spoke of grounded force; of churning, boiling, barely contained power and strength.

Each one strong and vicious enough to survive in the company of the other four, they were a dangerous company indeed. Starved of affection and often simply starved they had grown to love most the hard things in life. They lived to fight and to kill, loved the warm taste of blood and savoured hard struggle.

They were comrades and competitors- steel sharpened by steel and they were fixed on Ellie with fatal intent.

Ellie ran. There was no way she would outrun these animals ultimately but she should not fight them here in the open. If she got to the forest she would be at a reduced disadvantage. That was her kind of world and the lack of space between the trunks of the densely packed trees would make it more difficult for her to be surrounded.

As she ran she found herself thinking how strange it was that these powerful dogs could be controlled by humans who were so much weaker. It was strange but she knew it was true. She had seen it herself. Now was not the time for such musings. She pulled her mind back to the here-and-now.

The dogs were making up ground on her all the time, no matter how swiftly she ran they would always be faster, but she made it to the forest before they could run her down and they were a little spread out now as they did not all run at the same pace. This and the change of the environment were in Ellie's favour. She was gradually reducing the odds against her, even if it was only by a little.

The leading dog was snapping at her heels when she leapt into the first large tree she came to but there was a little distance between him and the others now. Instead of climbing the tree to safety Ellie launched herself backwards from it and dropped onto the dog's long back. She wound her arm around the dog's neck and clasped her legs around him to keep her in place. She squeezed and crushed with all her might. It had to be quick. She pulled up with her shoulders and down sharply with her hips.

The dog's neck was broken and Ellie had sped off among the trees in the time it took for the other dogs to catch up.

They spent only a moment acknowledging the death of the one who had been the most dominant among them. It caused them no fear, it did not make them rethink their purpose, it only caused more excitement and then they were back to the chase as full of deadly intent as before.

Ellie could already feel exhaustion approaching. That, she knew, could bring death with it. She could not wait and let it take hold.

She climbed the tallest tree she could find quickly. She climbed high and fast without looking back. The dogs found her easily by scent but they could not follow her. Their excitement grew with the feeling that they had their quarry trapped.

Above them Ellie surveyed the canopy of the forest around her. She could see a path through the trees. The branches were packed together, one tree reaching out and touching the next. She could travel for a long distance up here if she wanted to, moving from tree to tree.

She set off and the dogs followed her on the ground- furious, frustrated but with no loss of determination. They would make her pay for this frustration when they eventually brought her to their teeth.

From her high vantage Ellie could not only travel but she could also see much of the land below and she was determined to make it a weapon.

The dogs followed her relentlessly, directing on her a fierce focus. After more than two hours of this game of cat and mouse Ellie saw something that quickened her pulse.

Ahead on the path the dogs were travelling was a large, hollow, fallen tree. Ellie knew that this was just the sort of place large constrictor snakes liked to make their homes. She searched the area with her eyes. The heavy, dragging marks she saw near the tree made her almost certain that a large predatory snake lived there. It was worth the chance, it was well worth the chance.

She descended to a level that made the dogs feel that their opportunity to reach her might have come and began shouting at them, mocking them, calling them weak and stupid four-legged fools.

They barked and howled and leapt up at her.

When she knew they were blind with rage and aggression she started moving forward again. The dogs followed in a frenzy of noise and hatred and they ran headlong against and over and through the fallen tree where Ellie had been leading them.

As they pushed onwards a large, silent head emerged from the ruin of the trunk and struck out like lightening at the dog taking up the rear, one of the two black ones. The snake latched onto the dog and gripped hard. The dog tried to spin and fight back but the snake, whose body was still emerging from the tree, so large was it, so immensely strong, was too much. It twisted and spun violently and swept the dog onto its back. This canine killer had more than met its match. He would fight to the end, he would injure the snake but, there was no doubt, he would be defeated.

Ellie looked back only long enough to see the two animals locked in a struggle to the death. See could see that the reptile already had the advantage and would certainly prevail but that was not important to her. What was important was that the dog, win or lose, would not come out of the encounter a continued threat to her.

She moved on as fast as she could, creating distance between the three remaining dogs and their doomed fellow as quickly as she could.

They followed her all that day. She slept in the canopy of the trees that night, hungry, tired but safe.

The dogs watched, sleepless all night, their will to destroy her undiminished. Ellie knew that their will could never be broken. The dogs would die before they broke off from their goal. Still, she was safe for now and she was able to relax her body and rest enough to help her prepare for the trials to follow.

When the morning came Ellie began to move again. The dogs followed her like murderous shadows.

Soon she spied something very familiar to her, painfully so. It was a large mound of earth, leaves and twigs. It looked soft but she knew if you looked closely you would see the thousands of army ants that had made their home there.

She led the dogs in its direction- throwing small branches at them and yelling again to make sure they had no hint as to what she was leading them towards.

Soon the smallest of the dogs was jumping in circles, biting at his own flesh, wondering in a panic what was happening to him as his skin burned and stung in a hundred different places at once.

Ellie pushed on, moving above the forest floor with her confidence beginning to grow. She was followed now by only two pursuers. She thought about trying her luck in a fight with them but the risk seemed still too great. She would have to remain patient for now, lead them on and look for her opportunities to further turn the tables on them.

About noon, she came towards a gap in the trees that opened to reveal a wide river. She had finally run out of space. The dogs knew it and their excitement rose.

Ellie scanned the river. It was muddy and dark. It moved slowly enough to swim but the dogs could surely swim it too, she would not want to fight them in the water.

She watched and thought and considered until she saw something break the surface of the river. She peered and studied how it moved, the subtle wake of it just below the water's surface and soon she recognized it. It was the head of a monitor lizard. These lizards were big, carnivorous and aggressive but she knew how they hunted and she knew that she could use that knowledge to her advantage.

She jumped out of the tree and sprinted for the river. The dogs tore after her, gaining ground with every step. When she reached the river she launched herself in and immediately propelled herself under the surface of the water.

The monitor lizard likes to hunt at the surface, picking its prey from the place where the water meets the air. If she could swim the breadth of the river without surfacing she should be safe.

The dogs, however, could not do that. They would swim in exactly the position that triggered the lizard to attack.

Ellie silently thanked the Crocodile for all the hard lessons in breath control as she pushed strongly through the current. She felt things moving close to her and past her but concentrated on just making progress.

When she left the river on the far shore she turned quickly to see what would confront her. Following after her was only one dog. The water made his fur even darker in parts while in other parts he was covered by mud and what Ellie hoped was his own blood.

The dog did not care. He seemed not to even notice that he was the last one remaining on the hunt. At last he had his prey and the prey was all his now. Numbers would make no difference.

He needed no companions; he wanted no advantages. He himself was the advantage, this was the reason he lived. He paused a moment to enjoy the taste of fear that was carried on the air from the girl to him.

Ellie already knew she had to face the dog down. There was no safety for her to run to, no strategy to employ beyond the strategy of the fight. She had played her tricks and played them well but she was left with one more mountain to climb.

"Stay away from the jaws, stay away from the teeth," she whispered to herself and then they closed on each other.

He lunged forward, low and hard, meaning to take her low on the legs and bring her to the ground where her throat would be within reach of his bite. Ellie threw her hips back and pushed down hard on the back of his head, pushing it forcefully into the earth as she circled off, striking a blow behind his ear as she moved away and turned to face him again.

The dog was pleased. The blow had barely hurt him but at least he would have a little challenge. They closed on each other again. The dog sprang at her, higher this time, going straight for the neck. Ellie moved a little too slowly and as she tried to side step she was caught on the shoulder by the dog's weight and she was spun to the ground. She jumped back to her feet a split second before the dog snapped his jaws shut less than an inch from her leg.

She was losing energy, nearing exhaustion and her opponent was feeling strong, able to go on like this for as long as it took.

Ellie saw a rock close enough to grab. A head on attack, even with a weapon was not likely to go well for her but if she continued in this way she would simply be overtaken by exhaustion and the dog would have his victory. She would take the small chance over no chance at all. She dashed to the rock as the dog sprinted to intercept. She reached it just as the dog leapt towards her, jaws gaping. She swung around and drove the rock forwards with everything she had left into the dog's skull.

There was a dreadful crushing sound and a high-pitched jip and then the dog fell at her feet. Blood was already flowing freely from a wound in its head. Ellie approached the prone beast with the rock raised but it made no move. She stood frozen for a long time before she dropped the rock and slumped to the ground.

It was over. She was safe; for the moment. Until her adrenalin began to wear off she could not completely accept that. She turned her head from side to side checking for the next attack. It didn't come. She checked herself over to see if she was seriously hurt. She was bruised and scratched and it looked like the dog had opened two larger but not dangerous cuts on her left forearm. They would need to be treated but that was not urgent. Now she needed to find her way home. She had all she would need to recover in the garden and in her own small alcove. Rest, good food and herbs were waiting for her there.

She set off. It was not difficult for her to find her way. All the time she expected a new attack; some new danger but it didn't come. Soon she was relaxing into practices of path-finding and navigating that were as natural and familiar to her as waking up in the morning. She found her way with confidence back to land she knew, felt its homely reassurance under her feet like a friend helping her onwards.

It took time but eventually she was in sight of her lake. She moved faster, opening up her stride. She tried to keep her excitement in check, not to rush blindly forward; but her heart was lifting with joy. She realised that she loved this place, that it was truly her home, her safe place. She approached the edge of the forest and could smell her cave.

Then she heard the voice. A deep and commanding voice. Most strangely of all, it was a human voice-

"Go back,"

It said.

"Go back, you are not wanted here."

Blocking the entrance to HER cave she saw a man. He was tall and supple like a hare. He was muscular like an ape. His eyes were cold and focused like those of a crocodile.

His shoulders and neck swelled with power like a hyena.
He had the intimidating presence of a wolf.

"Go back now," he growled.

"I have nowhere else to go," Ellie stood her ground.
"This place is my place."

"No, this place is mine. I was raised here and I claim
it."

What was this man saying? It could have been her saying
these words.

He did not give her time to consider.

"Go back or die here." He threw the words down as an
ultimatum.

"I told you, this is my home."

Ellie moved forward. She knew there was no point in
talking any more. This was part of the test. No matter
how fatigued she felt; no matter how much pain and
confusion she felt, this was something she would have to
do.

The man smiled bitterly as he also moved forward. His expression suggested a secret being held in reserve, ready for the right moment to be revealed.

His stance, bent at the knees with his weight over his leading leg, told Ellie that he was looking for grips- that he intended to grapple. She sunk her own weight lower and made ready to throw her own hips back to deny him those grips if necessary.

Then there was a flash, Ellie felt her legs collapse and her body hit the ground. She managed to hold on to consciousness but by her fingertips only. She had not seen the punch coming. He had perfectly sold her the fake.

See could see that his smile had grown from where she was looking up at him from below. But he had not pressed home his advantage. He was wasting crucial moments enjoying his work before his work was completed. That was a weakness and it had not been hidden from her.

She placed one hand on the earth and pulled one leg backwards keeping her eyes fixed on his the whole time.

She held an arm out to control the distance between them and snapped back to her feet.

He circled her and she followed; not allowing him to create an angle of attack against her. He flashed a lead hand and followed with a low kick to her lead thigh. His ankle thudded into the meat of her upper leg, making a deep sound and sending a sickening pain through Ellie's whole body. If she took too many of these strikes she would not be able to use that leg. She would not be able to move, it would be enough to decide the outcome of this battle.

The man continued to circle her, like a predator who has noticed his prey is injured and weakening, who is confident that he only needs to be patient and continue on his course to achieve his ultimate goal.

Another kick hit home. Ellie was already beginning to limp. Her time was running out with every painful and difficult step she took.

She tried to draw him into strikes of her own but he seemed totally in control. It felt like he could read her mind. He knew every move she would make before she made it.

He had been trained by the same teachers who had trained her.

She felt his hip twitch a split second before his next kick. She threw herself forward and grabbed his foot. At the same time she pushed as powerfully as she could through his shoulder and they both tumbled to the ground.

He was larger and stronger than her and she knew it would be near impossible to hold him down. She would have to allow him to move but just enough to take advantage of this scramble and use it to find an opportunity to finish the fight.

Every moment they contended was draining Ellie of energy she could not spare and if she allowed this fight to go on she would lose to exhaustion as surely as she might lose to her human opponent.

She lifted her weight from him a little. He immediately started to posture upwards, trying to get back to his feet. She moved fluidly past the shield of his legs and wrapped an arm around his neck. She clasped her hands together and pulled back.

He exploded. Turning her onto her back. She held on with arms and legs and continued to put pressure on his neck. As he fought to pull his head free she made tiny adjustments to the position of her wrists, working them deeper and deeper into the flesh of his throat.

He was breathing with some difficulty now, beginning to realise that he was in real trouble. He lifted her from the ground and slammed her back down. She felt the impact rattle through her, shaking her bones, threatening her grip but she held on and squeezed tighter.

He lost consciousness first and for a moment she considered releasing her grip. She wanted to do so, she wanted to talk to this man, find out who he was and question him about what must have been their shared experiences, but she didn't. She understood that this fight was not one she was allowed to stop when she wanted to- it was a fight to the end.

She held on with all she was worth and the end came.

Chapter 17

Exhausted and feeling quite empty inside Ellie entered her cave and found it transformed. It was larger and damper. Lit by blazing torches. It was a different place. She had been here before, long ago. At the beginning. The struggles of the previous two days had drained her of her capacity to be shocked. She simply walked forward and looked around her.

The animals were all there, all of them. All the creatures she knew and who had been her teachers and many, many more. Animals that still walked the earth outside these caves and ones that had long since ceased to. Beautiful and terrifying combinations of beaks and claws and wings and paws and teeth and tails; short legs and long legs; tall, squat, fast or powerful, predators with eyes facing forward and the anxious, side-facing eyes of prey. Animals that ran or leapt or climbed or swam. Animals that loved the high cold mountains or the hot, dry plains and deserts.

The musty mixed up smells of huge animals hung in the air in a thick cloud. She saw the Hyena watching her with something like a cross between relief and shame in her eyes. The Hare was looking anxious. The Ape held an intense, serious expression but she could see it was forced, hard for him to hold on his face. As usual she could read nothing from the eyes of the Crocodile.

The Wolf came forward from the crowd, walking slowly and steadily. He spoke in a deep and sombre tone-

"The old go to the teeth of the young," he intoned in his deep, serious voice.

He crossed to her and licked the blood from her face and hands.

Ellie herself, was full of questions and rage. Her empty feeling had been replaced with anger and the need for answers. She was done with being controlled, finished with being a pawn in a game she didn't understand.

She fixed the Wolf with a hard stare and was about to challenge him; she knew she would be destroyed but she didn't care any more. Just as she was about to raise her voice, the Wolf cut her off.

"Now you learn who and what you have become."

Whatever words she had been about to say died in her throat.

"Now it is time for your questions to be answered. Listen and be silent. This story is long and some of it will be beyond your ability to comprehend but listen and you will learn enough now and later it is possible that you will understand more and more.

About forty thousand human years ago the first great extinction started. It started on the huge island that was Australia and New Guinea before those land masses separated. They, the humans, killed all the giant lizards, the great marsupials, leopards and rhino, the giant birds and kangaroos. The great ones, the archetypes. The original bearers of the names.

Since then, all over the world it has continued-Eurasia, Africa, Asia. The giant geese of Hawaii, the great lemurs of Madagascar. We animals have been getting smaller both in size and number as we have been afforded less and less space in which to live.

Even a type of human they call Neanderthal, their own kind, they killed off systematically.

We have seen these events, we were born from them, from the constant stream of these deaths. The pain and the murder flowed like a river, growing stronger and more forceful and bursting into a huge ocean. We were born from that ocean. We have grown stronger and larger with history. As we have become smaller and smaller, weaker and weaker in one world; we have become stronger, larger, more powerful in another.

For some time we have been working in the human world. Using agents like you and the man you have just killed to punish and dissuade. You can go where we cannot. You can move among them. You can take revenge and plant in their minds a certain hesitation. Until the time comes for us to take back entirely what they have wasted and spoiled, you can be our agent in their world and they can never be easy in their evil..."

And so Ellie began to learn who she had become and what was expected of her. She was an assassin. Her job was to go where her mentors sent her and punish those she was instructed to punish. She had slowly been learning all the skills she needed to do this job perfectly.

With time and contemplation she did not feel sad or guilty about this role. She felt as if she was doing what she was meant to do. She felt like a force of nature. She felt like a storm that washes away what is unclean.

She was sent on missions around the world. In the course of two years she built up a fearsome but secret resumé of violence. The world had almost no hint of her existence. She was like a predator that moves in the dark of the night and is known only, if at all, by the sudden destruction of her prey.

Chapter 18

In the most eastern part of Eastern Europe there is a country called Moldova. It is a small country and by most of the ways these things are measured it is the poorest nation in the whole of the continent.

It sits between Romania and the Ukraine, two much larger countries and it is a little squeezed in there. Ellie understood all this and understood how it worked to her advantage.

It was easier for her to operate in countries like Moldova because the police force was underpaid and disorganized, the different provinces unconnected and she could move more quickly than she could be tracked. It is tough for people who live in circumstances like this but it was the perfect environment for Ellie and that was all she cared about that.

Ellie had entered Moldova the previous day from Transnistria, a country that does not officially exist. It is there, however, a tiny territory run almost entirely by a single Russian gangster warlord whose presence is felt in the fact that all the shops,

businesses and apartment buildings carry the same name-
his name.

Transnistria was a monument to one man's ego but
equally it was an easy transit point for Ellie. She found
her way to the spot on the map the Wolf had directed her
to and she waited for her targets to arrive.

From Ellie's vantage point the scene was one of dust
and blood.

The day was hot. The sun was high in a cloudless sky. A
crowd of roughly thirty men circled a patch of dust
stained with gore and hair. Between fights the space was
cleared, quickly and not perfectly, so that the brown
clay became increasingly reddened with the blood of the
fighting dogs.

Ellie sat on a small hill downwind of the scene. She
could not be seen but she could see clearly all that she
needed. She was not angry and she was not fearful. She
saw nothing that would cause her to fail in her mission.
She was in a state of mind she thought of as 'hunting and
gathering'- hunting her prey and gathering the
information she needed to do her job.

From out of the crowd two men emerged from opposite sides leading a dog each on very thick, short leads. The dogs were quite small but extremely muscular. Waves of energy were pulsing along the chains of their muscles, all pounding blood and nervous excitement.

A wiry brown and white dog was led by a large man with a black beard. The other animal was black and led by a small man wearing sunglasses and sporting a shaven head.

Many people like to gamble. Some people; too many, like to gamble on death. They like the excitement of violence and danger. They like to feel powerful. They like to link through a wager to a drama they themselves would be afraid to become involved in. They become addicted to risk, at one remove, to blood sacrifice made to their own cowardice.

This is a perfect opportunity for criminals to profit. For those who are willing to trade-in their kindness, their compassion and their decency, there is money to be had and a temporary form of power. If your life has already robbed you of things like softness and compassion than this becomes easy to do.

Most are eaten up and spat out by this kind of life but some rise to a kind of corrupt success and pull the strings controlling situations like the dogfights Ellie was surveying from her high viewing point.

It would not have been easy to pick out the two men who were really in charge here. They were not holding dogs. They were not shouting and throwing money around. They were not expensively dressed. They were not the ones wearing t-shirts with the sleeves cut off to display their powerful arms. They were a quiet pair; a father and son.

The older man was in his sixties. He was wearing a white fedora hat to shield his eyes from the harsh sun. He had a white, short-sleeved shirt, ironed to perfection. His face was peaceful and calm, it even looked kind. He was an ordinary retired gentleman, someone's favourite grandfather perhaps.

The other man was in his forties. He had dark hair, balding in the centre. He was neither particularly big nor small. He was neatly and professionally dressed but more than anything else he looked altogether ordinary.

They seemed less weather beaten and less aged than many of the men around them. They touched no money and they seemed almost uninterested in the proceedings beyond shaking hands with each and every new arrival but all the gambling was operated by the organisation they controlled and everybody understood that.

Their protection was nearby; large, fit looking ex-military types who knew their business well. Ellie knew that they would probably have to go but the other two were her real targets. They would die today but not here. There were far too many people around.

Ellie drank in all the information she needed. Also, she saw the dogs set against each other and let loose. She saw them tear into each other with ferocity. She watched and thought about animals trained from pups to fight and to kill for someone else. Never having a choice, manipulated and exploited by beings that controlled their world as if by magic. That thought scared her when very little else did.

Near the edge of the patch of earth where the dogs were being made to fight Ellie saw a small group of jeeps. They were clean and well looked after. The drivers stayed near the jeeps. They looked as if they were armoured,

perhaps they had bulletproof glass. These would the
vehicles of the two men she was here to kill.

When the time was right and the afternoon was getting
old she made her way down the hill carefully and hid
herself in the trunk of one of the jeeps. And waited.
When Ellie emerged from the trunk of the jeep she found
herself between the back of a small building and the
entrance to a vineyard. The ground rose in a gentle slope
towards the descending sun. The world was glowing and
golden and somehow seemed inappropriately soft. She could
relax here if she were allowed.

Ellie moved around the edge of the building, staying
close to the walls like a stealthy rodent, and peered out
at the vineyard.

The old man was out there, absent-mindedly checking the
harvest, running a lazy hand over the plants. A ruthless
organised criminal acting the part of the dreamy
grandfather. Maybe he partly believed the lie himself at
that particular moment.

This would have been an excellent time to kill him but
for the fact that he was alone and it would possibly
alert everyone and make the second man harder to get to.

Ellie had two men to kill and she knew it was better not to draw out the process. She needed both of them in one place.

The old man looked at the setting sun for a few moments then turned sharply on his heels and went inside. Ellie cut the gentle images from her mind and went to look for another way to follow him.

Buildings like this old farmhouse were like the walls of mountains to her. She saw ways to climb up and to break in everywhere. They stood out under her gaze as though they were marked and numbered.

She jumped onto a small out-building, made her way across its flat roof and from there swung up to the sloped roof of the main building.

It was covered with large, clay tiles. They were light pink in colour and they glowed in the late evening sun. She explored their edges with her hands and soon found one that was loose. She prized it and two others up and looked inside. She had made herself an entrance into the dark eaves of the building. She dropped down softly.

She moved slowly and carefully until she could hear voices. She followed them and found a gap in the boards. Below her she could see something that might have been a painting. A happy family eating and talking together. There were the two men who were her targets, a woman, and two children. A little boy about five and a girl maybe two or three years younger than him.

It looked very like a restaurant, except this restaurant only had one table and that table was flanked by two armed men standing guard.

One man, acting as both chef and waiter came and went every now and then bringing fresh dishes, filling glasses of wine and cups of coffee for the adults and smaller cups of fruit juice for the children.

The guards and the waiter were so quiet and respectful it was almost like they were not there, as if they were invisible and there was just this family enjoying each other's company.

As Ellie watched them it became difficult for her to focus. She thought it might be the contrast between the darkness of the space around her and the bright open space below. Perhaps it was the little specks of dust floating in the air around her. In truth, it was neither of these things.

There was something both strange and familiar about what she was witnessing. It was stirring up memories of a different life. Something homely and unhomely at the same time. A memory of a home she wasn't sure was real. A memory that didn't fit into any easy place in her mind. A square memory in a round hole.

Ellie was beginning to feel dizzy. She shook her head and controlled her breath. She would do her work, she told herself. She would always do her work.

She moved across the ceiling until she was over the kitchen. Quickly she loosened three boards and dropped down behind the chef. She wrapped an arm around his fat neck and squeezed until he was asleep. She stopped. That was enough, he would stay out of action for as long as she needed him to. She found two large, sharp kitchen knives and weighed them in her hands. They were well balanced.

The two bodyguards could not be given the same treatment as the chef. She threw the knives and both of them fell. She sprang into the room, grabbed one of the guns and used it. Both her targets fell. She checked the bodyguards; neither was breathing. She began to relax a little.

Then she heard screaming. The terrified woman was shouting at her in a language she didn't understand and Ellie had a decent understanding of a lot of languages.

The woman stood trembling with her children protected behind her outstretched arms. In her left hand she held a large, sharp steak knife. Ellie had no interest in harming her or the children but she could see that the woman was panicked beyond reason and she did not want to turn her back on her as long as she held the knife. Someone in this state could easily lose control completely and attack. Not taking that threat seriously was a good way to get yourself killed.

It was easy to disarm the woman. Despite her passion and desperation she had no skill with which to confound a trained fighter like Ellie.

Ellie pinned her to the ground hoping she would see that there was nothing she could do and Ellie would be able to leave her and go. Then something hit her on her back. It was not heavy and not strong but it was full of energy and conviction. The little boy had rushed forward to defend his mother.

Ellie tore him from her back and threw him to the ground. She held him by the throat and one wrist, pinning him helplessly. She looked at the child beneath her and one word flashed in her mind:

"Tristan"

It exploded in her brain physically, painfully. She let go her grip and ran. She ran as though she were being chased by a beast more powerful than any she had ever encountered before and she ran for a long time, the movement of her body shielding her from something terrible in her mind.

As she fled she ran past the wall-mounted camera that had recorded everything and which she had failed to notice or disable.

# Part Two- The Dream of Home

Chapter 19

Wilhelmina Benjamin surveyed her desk through tired eyes and considered for easily the thousandth time just how very much she hated paperwork. Yes, she knew it was a cliché, the cop who hates paperwork, she had seen enough movies and read enough thrillers to be aware of that; but it also was, like a lot of clichés now that she thought of it, the truth.

The surface of her fairly large desk was covered with a worryingly large mountain range of documents and no matter how much work she put into reducing its height and breadth, it was only expanding.

Wasn't the world supposed to be 'going paperless'? We were supposed to be living in a world of digital communications weren't we? She had a computer, a tablet and a smartphone that she thought of as half-smart and half-dumb because it was always chasing its own tail trying to update something or other and becoming frozen in the process. All these gadgets were currently buried somewhere under the mountains of paper that met her every morning when she arrived at the office.

Soon, she would have to call in a team of archaeologists if she needed to locate, say, a keyboard or a mouse.

And the paper mountains just kept growing. It was this job- a lot of frustrating information with little satisfying explanation.

It had felt like a huge promotion when she was offered the job with Interpol, the European Police Agency, and she had imagined herself working on big drug smuggling cases, international art crime or terrorism but instead she had been given this strange and frustrating… 'project' was the best word.

She had understood when she took the job that Interpol doesn't actually investigate crimes on the ground but it does help local police forces to pool information and take the action they need to solve large international crimes. It gives you the chance to be a mastermind of investigations, making connections between individual crimes and revealing a bigger picture. It was a chance to become a really good detective, a Sherlock Holmes brilliantly seeing the important connections and shining a light on the solutions to seemingly unsolvable mysteries; but that was not the role she felt she was inhabiting at the moment.

The job she had been assigned to for the last nearly two years was not the sort she had imagined she would be working on when she had excitedly moved her life from Birmingham in England to Lyon in France where Interpol has its headquarters.

Her brief was vague and hard to explain; in fact, she tried to spend as little time as possible explaining it to anyone. When old colleagues, friends or family expressed an interest in what she was investigating she would start to tell her story and watch as their eyes first narrowed in confusion, then rolled back with boredom.

It was not worth the annoyance so she had stopped talking about it. That actually made some people more curious, which made them ask more often, which was more annoying for Wilhelmina.

Even her present colleagues were unsure of what exactly she did. This made her feel like the odd-one-out in the office. She had climbed all the way up to Interpol and it was still just like being in school in that way. She was still the slightly weird outsider.

The best way she could summarize it; and she had worked hard on this (like doing an essay in school, school again!) her assignment was this:

Someone, some bright spark, had noticed two brutally violent crimes, one in Belgium and another in Hungary that had no apparent connection except that both seemed to involve punishing criminals for the abuse of animals. However, no animal rights group had claimed responsibility, no statements were made and the crimes were carried out with an expertise that if anything suggested military involvement. So this was all she had-

1 Animals being abused in some way
2 Extreme but seemingly expert violence
3 No messages of responsibility, no group looking for publicity
4 Some basic physical evidence that led nowhere. No fingerprints or hair samples that matched with anything on any database
5 No witnesses

Then someone noticed some more of these crimes. At about that same time she arrived in the Interpol offices, wide-eyed and excited, someone high up had decided it would be a good idea to pass this headache onto the new girl. If there was a connection between all these incidents maybe she could find it, if not, it was no great loss. In that sense it had been just a case of bad timing. She had walked in the door just in time to catch the case that no one who had been there longer wanted to touch.

Once someone had been put in charge of this problem it had grown and grown. It was impossible to tell which incidents that came to land on her desk were part of her case and which were not since it was impossible to tell what the case actually was. It was like trying to wrestle a ghost, it kept shifting its shape and disappearing from view just when she tried to focus hardest on it.

Her colleagues had begun to refer to her as 'La dame des animaux', 'The animal lady'; not in a nasty way but she didn't like the pigeonhole it placed her in and worse still she couldn't find a way out of it.

The incidents themselves were deeply upsetting as well as frustrating, like the one that  had recently been brought to her attention from Thailand. There were three men, ex-military, known criminals and hard men, dead in a garage in Chiang Mai. The garage had been a front for any number of criminal activities. One of them, and this was the reason Wilhelmina was reading about it, was the warehousing of wild animals that were later sold as pets.

There had been a room in the back of the garage full of cages in which these animals were being kept and all the animals had themselves also been killed.

This was not uncommon in these incidents. It was as if whoever had killed the three men had made the practical determination that there was no way to release the animals back into the wild and therefore it would be better for them to die. If that was the case, it was a very hard and chilling logic. Whoever had committed this crime had a very cold and very dangerous determination.

If the same person, or group of people were responsible for all or most of these crimes, they would be very scary people indeed. If that were the truth and if she were to help to stop them, well that was a lot of 'ifs' as her father used to say to her when she was a child and feeling anxious over some imagined disaster that might befall her 'if'.

She was not going to Thailand, there was not money in the expenses for that but she had the paperwork to pour over, and over, and over again.

She threw the file back with the others and decided it was time for an early lunch. She did not often take early lunches, being in general a stickler for punctuality and doing things 'the right way' but today she felt worn down enough to make an exception.

There were not all that many places for a vegetarian to eat in Lyon but she was informed by her French colleagues it had been a lot worse not so very long ago. For lunch she often visited a Middle Eastern place called Yaafa which was not specifically veggie but due to the nature of Middle Eastern cuisine naturally had lots of dishes she could eat.

She preferred not to eat in solely vegetarian places anyway as she liked to feel that it was possible for people to hold strong convictions without losing sight of the possibility that they might be wrong or at least might not tell the full story; she liked to think that responsible people could disagree and get along respectfully.

This instinct may have been a result of her background, growing up with a Jamaican father and Irish mother (both second generation) in Birmingham, she found the mixing of cultures and ideas very natural. On the other hand, no one likes to think their personality can be explained so easily and Wilhelmina liked to think there was certainly more to it than that.

She bought her falafel from Ariel, who ran and part owned Yaafa and then brought her food and a soya mocha out to sit by the river.

She was still thinking about the three men dead in that garage in Chiang Mai. She didn't mind obsessing about work in the normal run of things, in fact she was proud of it, but that was when there was some positive direction of travel, a goal and a reasonable possibility of reaching it through her own efforts. This was different.

For one thing, she found it very easy to let her mind, usually a very rational implement during office hours, slip to the supernatural when she considered these killings. She found herself creating an image of some sort of precisely directed werewolf or some such silly thing or other. This was not how, by nature or training, she was inclined to think when it came to work.

Both her father, the policeman, and her mother, the accountant, were fluent and fascinating storytellers. Her early childhood memories were made up as much of the fictions they had woven for her and her brother as they were of actual events. This had its advantages and disadvantages. She would not have given up 'for all the tea in China' her memories of the exploits of Jamaican and African trickster animals and the endlessly complex and intertwining stories of ancient Irish heroes and cattle raids. They had given her some nightmares though and they had given her a fictionalizing habit that would never disappear. Despite herself- she liked to make up stories. Some day she would enjoy telling those stories, along with the ones inherited from Mum and Dad, to her own kids. Perhaps.

On the other hand, she had never had a problem separating the logic and reason necessary to do her job successfully from her love of fiction.

Until now.

These crimes strongly felt like they were part of a very violent and dangerous fairytale. They represented a disturbing intersection of the realms of reality and the imagination; two worlds that only made good neighbours if they were clearly defined by good, strong fences.

She looked out over the river and tried to relax and enjoy her lunch. She should try that deep breathing thing her friend Jules was always talking about. She was not going to solve anything today.

Chapter 20

Marcus-

A pantry is a cool and comfortable place. It is a small room in which you keep your food stores. A pantry was a common room in houses before the invention of the refrigerator. After that it became something of a forgotten room, a waste of space. Its usefulness was gone but it is the way of things, important and unimportant, that they come round again. Things that lose their use value may well become fashionable in time. So with the pantry; it became something of a luxury, an extra room for those who could afford it; a status symbol. There are rules to a good pantry. For instance, it should ideally face north so that it remains cool all year round.

Marcus had loved that his family home in the country had a pantry. A little room, next to the kitchen and down a pair of narrow, stone steps, filled with shelves of good food on both sides and yes, north facing. A pantry, he would have told you, was a pleasant and comforting haven. Its presence in his home had been an image of the good and comfortable life he had made with Harriet for themselves and their children.

At this moment Marcus was huddled in a messy heap in a corner of his pantry sobbing and he had no intention of moving anytime soon, or ever again if he had his way.

It was the first of November. November is the month of memories. As the world outside grows darker vision turns inwards and the grainy films of our past that are always playing somewhere down deep inside us are pulled into a sharper focus that demands our attention.

It is easy to get swept up in November memories if they are pleasant but if they are bad, or worse, painful, it is all too easy to drown in them. Marcus was finding it nearly impossible to stay afloat as he sat, facing north, on the hard floor of the small, cold room.

After his daughter had disappeared Marcus's life had ended. He had been ashamed for years to admit this to the world or to himself. He had a wife and a son who he loved dearly and he had responsibilities to them. They should have been sweet responsibilities but the truth was that he died in some significant way after Ellie left his life and there was nothing he could do about it.

Years of pretending otherwise had left him exhausted and now, in the pantry of the house he used to love his energy had given out completely.

So he sat in a heap on the cold stone floor.

He didn't have the energy or desire to get up. Tristan stayed with him every second weekend and the other weekends were hard to get through, very hard. The long hours and minutes could not be entirely filled with work taken home from the office and housework. He would clean the house from top to bottom, scrub the whole place spotless. Then make a mess of it again as he ate his way through the rest of the day, tearing packets of biscuits and cereal bars out of their packets and devouring them without tasting a single bite.

After a while he didn't even notice that he was eating. He could stuff his face for hours until he suddenly became aware of himself. Then he cleared up the mess he had made and started over. All the while he thought of Ellie.

He would end up feeling dreadfully sick, collapsed on the couch or on the kitchen floor or, like now, on the pantry floor; feeling empty despite all the food.

"Eighty percent of children abducted in this way are killed within the first five hours. Most of the rest are murdered within the first twenty-four hours."

Marcus could not remember where he had heard or read that statement first. Strange how it remained burnt into his mind since the first moment and yet he couldn't remember when that was.

That was how Marcus's mind worked now and had worked, or not worked, since the day Ellie disappeared. It was a large, vague cloud with specific moments scorched into it with absolute perfect clarity. Deep in the mist of his mind, at the very centre of it was the one event. The one event that was the cause of everything and which could never be approached too nearly.

"Eighty percent of children abducted in this way are killed within the first five hours. Most of the rest are murdered within the first twenty-four hours."

The numbers made it feel horribly undeniable: Eighty percent, five hours, twenty-four hours. Simple numbers that said his daughter was dead.

The formality of the word 'abducted' bothered him hugely. 'Killed' and 'murdered'- there was no getting around the awful, blunt, basic, simplicity of those words.

All these words and numbers were like a fence around the one thing that was too awful to look at head-on. His whole life orbited around that moment on the beach when he had realised Ellie was really gone. So much of himself was still right there and still totally helpless.

It was a long time until he would have Tristan again and he was exhausted. He was exhausted right down to his bones.

Chapter 21

Harriet-

Harriet hated the Tube. The underground train system was the best, most efficient way for her to get to work but she genuinely loathed it.

She could walk to the station in five minutes, the journey took under fifteen, and then a five minute walk the other side. A bus would take far, far longer, stuck in traffic most of the time. The walk through London wasn't exactly pretty or inspiring and it was too long. It saw her arrive in work a hot and bothered mess.

Since she had moved back to London she despised the Tube because she could not stand to be trapped underground for any length of time. At night she had nightmares of being trapped in a cave. She woke up choking.

Yes, The Tube was by far the best way to go, she could read, listen to music, collect her thoughts. But her thoughts were the problem. They were difficult and she didn't want to collect them. Let them scatter and be blown away like leaves in the wind, that would suit her just fine.

Really she had to admit that nothing made her happy; everything was wrong one way or another. Since Ellie's disappearance every step that she took felt like too much work, every meal that she ate was tasteless, every conversation she had was pointless, every legal case she took was a waste of time and effort. Almost nothing felt like it had importance or meaning.

Only Tristan kept her going, only he was really important.

She hated to acknowledge it but Marcus was not enough to keep her going. For years now she felt like she was looking at him down the wrong end of a telescope. Whenever she met him he seemed to be receding further and further into the distance. He was like a tiny dot, too far away to reach out and touch.

As he had become smaller and smaller in her sight he had in fact become larger, rounder and softer in his person. She felt that something about his softness of body reflected a weakness in his character that she could not look at without a feeling of anger, and worse, disgust.

All of this played constantly in her mind. The thoughts tumbled and turned in circles and head over heels. Her head was never quiet, it buzzed like a hornets' nest. She couldn't sleep, when she did the nightmares came, she couldn't concentrate on any one thing for long; she was anxious all the time. It never gave her any rest and, of course, she could not talk to anyone about it. After a certain point, people, even those closest to you, even the kindest and most sympathetic, could not stand to hear a story like hers. It was not because it was so sad or so shocking, it was because it never improved, she never felt any better. The one thing that people cannot stand to be forced to think about is a pain that never gets better.

And Harriet did not want to feel better. Deep down she felt that would be a betrayal of her daughter.

The Tube just made it worse- like trying to stuff all those angry hornets into a small tin box, it simply amplified the din.

The best thing was for her to stay busy- work, look after her son, walk quickly to and from work, pace the floor when it was late at night and she was unable to sleep.

They had not done enough. If they had done enough they would have found their daughter therefore they had not done enough.

The local police had tried their best. The British police had done their best too when they had eventually become involved. The beach and the woods had been searched and searched again. Hundreds of people, then thousands of people were questioned, anyone and everyone who had been or could have been in the area from which Ellie had disappeared. Appeals for information had been made and rewards had been offered. False leads had been chased up and had brought them to a hundred dead ends.

Newspaper articles had been written about them. Initially sympathetic, after some time the opinion pieces suggesting they must have been neglectful parents began. In a surprisingly short time articles suggesting she and Marcus may have murdered Ellie appeared.

They were themselves questioned and investigated. Horrible, humiliating sessions breaking down every detail of their actions that day and later of their lives and characters. Worst of all, these suspicions about them were wasting time and removing focus from the real investigation.

And in the end it was no good. They could not find Ellie. They had to go back to work. They had to look after Tristan and pay bills. Their efforts to keep the search for Ellie going required money after all.

They never gave up of course. They did everything that they could to keep the case alive and they always would but then there was Marcus's horrible quote-

"Eighty percent of all children..." She shook her head, trying to cast the tormenting thoughts from her mind.

Chapter 22

Tristan-

"The Morden Academy School of Arts and Science"

That's what it said on the gate that Tristan Burnham was walking through on his third day at his third school since he and his mother had moved back to London.

He was already not popular with either the teachers or his fellow students and he already didn't care. In fact, he hadn't cared since before his first day.

He was listening to a Danish Hardcore band called "Iceage" through his headphones. The song was called "Morals" and he was lost in its dense waves of noise; getting the most out of the little time he had left before he would have to return to the equally dense but far more complex and troubling world of school.

Tristan barely noticed Matthew Dunne and John Caton as he passed them by. These two had already made it known that they had taken a dislike to him. They were popular boys and could turn others against him no doubt but so be it. Tristan had been of the opinion for some time that the quicker he was established as unpopular and an outsider, the better it was. He was not looking to make friends. For friends he had music, books and podcasts; beyond that what he wanted most was to be left alone.

Something caught Tristan low on his right leg. He made three or four tripping steps forward regaining his balance but he did not fall.  He turned to see Matthew and John laughing. Then Matthew was speaking. His face was all screwed up and aggressive and he was talking but Tristan couldn't hear what he was saying over the music in his ears. Tristan stared at Matthew watching his mouth move but hearing only the lyrics- "Where are your morals" over and over as the chorus of the song continued.

Clearly frustrated, Matthew stepped forward and pushed Tristan in the chest. Tristan removed his headphones and set his jaw.

When he was pulled off Matthew by Mr. Petrov from gym, Tristan was genuinely surprised to find that the other boy was bleeding from his nose and Mr. Murphy, the balding geography teacher, was carefully helping him to his feet. As he was dragged away to the school building he could hear a shocked John Caton saying, "We were just playing around, he's a psycho, he's a freak…"

They would not play that joke again, Tristan thought.

Mr. Petrov was a big man and Tristan was small for his age so it was easy for the teacher to carry the boy like an awkwardly shaped bag into the almost empty staff room. It was a strange feeling for Tristan to be carried like that, but he didn't fight. His adrenalin was wearing off and he was beginning to feel deflated, as he always did after a fight.

"This is your third day, only your third day," Mr. Petrov still had a strong accent from his native Bulgaria despite having lived in London for twenty years. He was peering with exaggerated concentration through his reading glasses at the school's notes re: one Tristan Burnham. Then looking over his glasses at the boy himself. An angry little fellow with a hard, defiant look pasted on his pale face.

He had read the notes already. He liked to know what trouble might be coming before it came. After today's incident he might not be able to keep the boy in the school but he was going to try. The story the notes told made him feel the lad deserved a chance.

About eight years ago his sister had gone missing when the family were on a dream holiday in Thailand. As you might expect everything had gone downhill from there for the whole family. His sister had simply disappeared from a beach, become an absence that destroyed everything else around it.

The media became interested of course and it became a huge story on television and the newspapers. At first, there was sympathy for the family but then a sense that the parents must have been in some way neglectful crept in.

Then the sympathy started to dissipate and the feeling of public anger against the parents grew. Some said they must have killed their daughter and tried to cover it up.

After a year or so the media stopped caring and the family were left alone to their misery and devastation. Every now and then the case came up in the press if someone thought they had seen the girl. CCTV camera shots were compared to computer-generated images of "what she would look like now". The girl was never found but the wound was kept fresh.

Three years ago the parents had split up and the boy moved back to London with his mother; the father was in Dorset according to the notes.

The official record missed out several important things. They didn't record the hole in his heart that Tristan felt every day and that it was impossible to fill; they ignored the difficulty he experienced getting to sleep every night; the dreams he had- anxious, confusing and terrifying dreams of a girl in a cave, sometimes alone and sometimes surrounded by strange, ghostly beasts.

The boy, who had been troubled before, became even more difficult and angry after the move to the city. He was uprooted. He didn't fit in anywhere and so he decided that he didn't want to. He was the cause of no trouble as he saw it but he was an obvious target for bullies and he was in the habit of meeting violence with more violence.

In truth, Mr. Petrov's note reading was partly an act designed to help him play for time; letting the boy's energy dissipate a little more and deciding how to handle this situation. Mr. Petrov strongly believed that boys were like dogs, though he would not have said that out loud in the staff room or to their parents. He found that both boys and dogs worked best with the application of exercise, discipline and affection…, IN THAT ORDER and that both dogs and boys should be actively engaged in something interesting or exhausted, or eating and that was pretty much that.

As with dogs, in Mr. Petrov's scheme of things, there was no point in trying to repair their behaviour unless and until they were in a calm state.

Tristan looked at the teacher. A gorilla of a man in a Mark and Spencer's suit with a big bald spot and reading glasses on a string. His shoulders rolled forward, bookending his massive chest. He wasn't smiling, of course, but it looked like he might not have his top two front teeth. Despite the details, the sum of its parts added up to a kindly face rather than an intimidating one.

Mr. Petrov looked back at the boy and made a decision.

Tristan was more tired than he had ever imagined it was possible to be. Every time he had used the word 'exhausted' in his life up to this point he had been wrong, oh so wrong. Now he was truly exhausted and he was happier than he had been in years. His t-shirt was soaked with sweat and he could barely move his weary limbs. He was a little light-headed but not at all in a nasty way. Steam was rising off him as if he were a melting volcano.

Around him on the gymnasium mats were about ten other men and boys and even a couple of girls.

When Mr. Petrov had suggested, strongly suggested, that Tristan channel his energy and his anger into a wrestling class the boy had not been sure at first if the big teacher was joking. He wondered if he was talking about the kind of professional wrestling he had seen on television that involved large men performing prearranged moves in outlandish spandex outfits. Tough; they really threw each other around but, Tristan thought, undignified. Mr. Petrov explained that he was talking about Greco-Roman and Freestyle wrestling.

"These are Olympic sports", he explained, "These are the oldest sports in the world. In the Bible Jacob wrestled an angel, or a creature that may have been an angel, and long before the Bible was written they described wrestling in the great epic poem 'Gilgamesh' and in the great Old English epic 'Beowulf'. Basically wrestling is an integral part of human culture and history. The whole world is about magic and wrestling. Here is the school of arts and science. Science is magic and wrestling is art."

This speech went on too long for Tristan's taste but he could see the guy was passionate about this stuff. Tristan himself was really not that interested but he understood that some effort on his part might keep him in this school and even though he didn't really care about that he further understood (all too well you might say) that his mother would be extremely unhappy if he got excluded from another school. He was running out of chances and really, he was very unhappy about upsetting his Mum.

Mr. Petrov, at the same time, was worrying that he may have gone too far with his little speech in terms of laying out how he personally felt the entire universe was organised but what was done was done. He wrote down the details of the class for Tristan and said- "Think about it." Then they went to the Head Teacher's office.

Tristan, still a student at the academy but only by the skin of his teeth, looked up this wrestling business on Youtube a couple of days later. He found video clips of men in funny looking singlets trying to throw each other around under a set of rules that was not quite clear to him. They were clearly fine athletes and tough but did he really want to spend his time doing this stuff…

Then he came across a clip of a Russian wrestler called Alexander Karelin. This man was the Incredible Hulk in real life. He was ridiculously big and powerful and he was shown lifting and slamming a series of other ridiculously big and powerful men as easily as Mr. Petrov had lifted Tristan. He seemed almost to be a creature from a different and distinct species. This was possibly the strongest, toughest human being who had ever lived.

Tristan changed his mind, "Go", "Don't go" several times a day between Mr. Petrov suggesting the class and the moment that his Mum got him into the car and took him to the school gym. Harriet had been all for anything that might help her son make some friends and do something social and positive, even though she was secretly a bit concerned about the getting thrown around part.

She left him at the door and told him she would be back for him in exactly two hours and he found himself nervously pushing his nose through the door into the hall.

The room was full of athletic looking people some of whom had misshapen noses and even stranger shaped ears. The room was uncomfortably hot and there was Mr. Petrov clearly in charge of all these formidable people.

The school allowed the teacher to run a wrestling class at the weekends but took no official interest in it beyond that.

Mr. Petrov saw him and beckoned him over.

"Just follow what we do Tristan. Anything you're nervous about just say. These people will look after you; they're not all that bad really."

And then to the room-

"This is Tristan Burnham. It's his first day so don't kill him ok."

The class began with a warm-up. After some stretching Tristan was paired up with one of the smaller men and they worked through a series of exercises together. This was very different from the warm-ups he was used to in gym class at school that involved little more than some lazy jogging on the spot. He had to carry the man up and down the mats on his back and then do the same journey holding the man in front of him, swinging him from hip to hip. It went on. By the end of the warm-up he was already really tired.

Then they ran through drills. They repeated throws and takedowns over and over again. Jim, Tristan's drilling partner explained a lot of technical details to him and made sure not to be too rough but even so it was difficult to deal with the fact that he was constantly being thrown to the ground. It was physically uncomfortable and it hurt his ego too.

At the end of the class they had ten minutes of sparring. Tristan was paired off with one of the girls. She was smaller than him and Tristan felt a little insulted.

The girl smiled and extended a hand. They shook and she introduced herself:

"Hi, I'm Ruth."

Tristan decided he would have to make a point with this girl. He wouldn't hurt her of course but he would have to show that he was made of more than this.

He squared up and tried to remember some of the throws he had drilled earlier.

Then he was in the air, not quite sure which way was up, and on his back a second later. He knew that he was supposed to stay off his back so he started to turn to his stomach, and his shoulder got slammed back to the floor with authority. He struggled to move but he was going nowhere. He had been pinned… by a girl.

It had taken about fifteen seconds.

They stood up and went at it again. This time Tristan remained on his feet slightly longer but he was soon travelling through the air again and landing on his back. Wherever he moved this girl made small adjustments to her weight distribution and he found himself even more immobile and trapped.

Then Ruth relaxed and stood up. She reached a hand out to help him up.

"Ok," she said, "Let's go again."

Afterwards Tristan found his mother waiting outside.

"You were a long time in there," she said with a smile.

Tristan looked at his watch, he had been training for nearly two and a half hours.

"Sorry," he said.

"Don't worry, it's fine. How was it?"

Tristan thought. It was good. It was embarrassing, extremely difficult, exhausting, but it was good. He felt better than he had felt in a long time. He felt calm.

"Not bad," he told Harriet, "I'll go again anyway." That night Tristan slept deeply and did not dream.

Chapter 23

Hungary-

Doctor Sabah Aziz walked alone in the fading light near the edge of the temporary camp where he had slept the previous night and where he would sleep in a small, cold tent that night again in a pattern that threatened to stretch long into his future.

He wished to get away from the noise and the smell for a short period- just a little break from the reality of his situation. His attempt would not, he knew, be very successful but he took some comfort from simply making the effort.

He felt older than his fifty years this evening- much older. He felt his age in the miles he had travelled to get here- which was nowhere; and the miles left to travel- which were many. He felt old all the way through his muscles, tired from walking and carrying his back pack, down to his bones and on down into his cells. He felt engulfed in exhaustion, it wrapped him up tightly like a blanket. That blanket could sometimes feel comfortable but it was a false friend that would trick you into quitting while there was still much left to do. The movement would help. Not much; but it would help, it usually did.

It had taken him months to get to Hungary from his home in Syria. He had travelled a long road through Turkey, Greece, Romania and Bulgaria. Bitterly, he thought of it sometimes as his 'grand tour'. He was seeing the world, just not in any way that he would have wanted to. He was part of a slowly moving train of human misery and anxiety.

He and his fellow refugees were almost numbed by the distances they had travelled and how far away hope still seemed. Still even moving slowly was better than being static, stuck in limbo. For the moment it seemed he was trapped in this camp so even a slow circuit or two at the perimeter fence was better than nothing.

The government here had mobilised the riot police to corral and control migrants and refugees like him as if they were a dangerous threat. Dr. Aziz was exhausted and hungry; he did not feel dangerous, he felt weak.

It was clear that the authorities here really did not have a definite idea of how to deal with them. They simultaneously did and did not want them to go forward and to go back. They pushed them together into a temporary camp with few facilities and left them there. Most of all, in their secret hearts, the politicians would like this messy lump of humanity to disappear or to never to have been; but they would not because they had little more than their stubborn clinging to basic existence remaining to keep them going.

Dr. Aziz felt this very strongly himself. He found himself looking out of the camp through the fence, past the police on guard and on down the road and simply thinking-

"I am here. I am a human being and I am not going away."

At other times the doctor felt the polite thing to do would be to disappear, save everyone the trouble, including himself; but he had not yet mastered that trick.

He had left his country when he ran out of hope and energy. Recognising that fact broke his heart. He had always thought of himself as strong but the war and the hospital had broken him. He did not want to dwell on that now. What good did it do anyone to wallow in despair? What help was that to the children he was no longer treating? They were still in the hospital in Aleppo along with Doctor Aziz's pride.

Here he was just a statistic- one of roughly five million Syrians who had fled the civil war in the previous five years. He had learned the hard lesson that so much of what he had fondly believed essential to him depended entirely on the life and the society he had grown up surrounded and nurtured by. When all of that had been torn down the doctor had been torn down too. What was left was not some essential, real him; it was a weaker, far less certain cartoon of his former self, a small child's drawing with fuzzy edges.

From the hope of the pro-democracy demonstrations in 2011, his country had collapsed into violence and civil war. The hospital where he worked had become a more and more desperate place until he no longer had the strength to witness the death and suffering that he could do so little to ease.

Having watched his society break down around him and then having left it all behind him to go where he was explicitly a stranger and an outsider he had found that he had already become that, a stranger to himself before he left home and the ghost's road through Europe was the right place for him.

It was so easy to become no one. In many ways he was composed mostly of memories now. He was a substantial biological being, a collection of limbs and bones, tissues and systems, standing on the earth under the sky, subject to the same laws of physics that ruled in Syria and everywhere else in the world. Why did he no longer feel real? For all of his rationalisations he could not adequately explain it to himself.

He began to hum an old song as he walked. It helped to calm him and bring him out of these sad and circular thoughts.

He heard a faint rustling in the bushes to his left. "Probably a rat," he thought. He was becoming quite comfortable with rats. The rats were often plump and healthy looking and he envied them their winter fat.

He continued on his slow, aimless walk. It seemed to him the rustling continued. It appeared to follow him. He stopped, turned and stared hard.

A girl emerged and stood meeting his gaze. Unfortunately it was nothing unusual to encounter a child travelling alone in these refugee caravans but there was something different about this girl.

She did not seem to be from any of the parts of the world that were sending people out in large numbers in search of a better life. She was tanned but she was obviously European. Beyond that there was something feral about her, like those children you read about who have been raised by dogs. She looked at him with the eyes of a suspicious animal.

"Hello," he addressed the wild girl in English. It was the language most likely to be understood. Most people on the road spoke at least a little and understood a little more.

"How are you young lady?" His English was school learned and formal. "More importantly- who are you?"

There was no answer.

"Ah," he continued, "so you are the quiet, mysterious type eh? I understand."

He began to walk slowly away. He resumed humming his old song.

After a few steps he glanced back over his shoulder and found the girl following. He spoke, just for the feeling of connection and communication which he was enjoying.

"When I was young, a little younger than you are now I think, they told a story in my district. They said that the leaves did not really fall off the trees."

He stopped and picked up a handful of wet leaves, turned them over thoughtfully in his hands and then let them fall gently to the ground.

"They said that ghosts moved into the attics of the houses in the winter and that they plucked the leaves from the trees to make themselves warm nests up there. They said you could hear them moving around at night. And it was true. You could definitely hear something moving around up there."

"I asked why there were so many leaves left on the ground and they said that ghosts are clumsy and have difficulty gripping."

"What do you think of that?"

The girl didn't answer but she was still following and he felt that she understood every word he was saying.

"Well, I thought they were perhaps trying to make a fool of me and I didn't like it. I was jealous of my dignity then. Later I thought perhaps they were just soft-headed old folks. Now, of course, all those people are themselves ghosts and I feel them with me all the time so they have proven their point, I think."

"I sometimes think that I am now a ghost also so I pick up a handful of leaves to test it. But then, as you saw, I can grasp them very well. With that I have no trouble."

"You know I think you understand me. I'm almost sure of that. Are you with anybody here?"

The girl still did not respond.

It was the children that broke his heart. His heart become harder in the last five years than he could have ever imagined it to be but the children broke it still. Every child he met like this one on the road reminded him of the ones he had cared for in the hospital. The confused and pain filled small faces were never far from his mind. He had no children of his own but the ones he cared for in the hospital had been his in an important way.

"Well, you have made it this far no matter what your circumstances. You'll need food. You can come with me if you like."

The girl showed no sign of moving.

"Well then, I can bring some to you."

The doctor went to his tent and put some porridge on the heat. Porridge was a Godsend here. It was simple to make and excellent at keeping the hunger at bay. He found his spoon and wiped it as clean as he could with a cloth he kept for that purpose only and which had become one of his most prized possessions, a treasured link to civilization and the softer life.

When the food was prepared he hurried back to the fence but the girl was gone.

Chapter 24

Ellie's journey to Hungary had been more direct and more secret than Doctor Aziz's. She had cut across the Ukraine and crossed the border unnoticed as was natural to her. She kept away from the main roads and routes and moved mostly through forests where she saw very few people and, lucky for them, none of them saw her.

Security around the Hungarian border had been tight but it was focused on finding large groups of refugees escaping war and poverty in Syria, Iraq, North Africa and more places. The more the police were concerned with them at the border the easier it was for Ellie to pass unseen. Ellie saw the men, women and children walking in lines along the sides of the roads with barely enough energy to keep going.

Ellie was not comfortable with weakness. Her own had been trained out of her. She watched these people walk with their heads down and an air of defeat about them with something like disgust mixed with a little sadness. It was the sadness that disturbed her for it was the sadness that was new.

Unlike the tired and hungry people being stopped on the border the journey had not been physically difficult for Ellie. She was trained so well that she could survive on her own for as long as she might need or want to; but the time had been filled with mental pain. Memories returning had tormented her with the miles.

Single words forced their way to the front of her mind. Names came back to her and faces followed. Stories and connections emerged from the fog of her past. She saw her mother, father and brother, clear and familiar. Family, her own family. She remembered who she was and where she was from.

The families on the roads; the tired adults and hungry children presented to her a mirror of the family she had lost.

She needed to go back to them. She needed to find her kin. It was not a comfortable feeling. It filled her with fear. Her logical mind told her that she was the soldier she had been for years. She had a defined and simple role. She was sharpened like a steel blade into the perfect instrument to fulfil that role. Against all that she felt the need to find these people and that place that had lain hidden inside her for so long. She felt it as a physical necessity. She would remain off balance until she met this need whatever it cost.

She knew she was betraying the creatures who had nurtured her for so long but it was also clear now that they had betrayed her, stolen something important from her and it was time for her to go and take it back.

She knew that she was from England. Her family would still be there. She would find them and give substance to the ghosts that were occupying such a large space in her mind. In that way she would get those ghosts out of her head.

After nearly two weeks she had come across the camp. As she had been trained to do she found a spot on high ground from which she could observe it without being seen herself. The camp was like an abandoned child. It was immature and struggling to find its feet in even the basic things. Were these people particularly incapable or unintelligent or were they somehow at an earlier stage in history. Men in uniform sometimes came and walked the perimeter of the fence. Sometimes they repaired damaged sections.

These people were- LIKE ANIMALS. The men in uniform were to be avoided, that would not be difficult, but the people inside the fence, they were more interesting than threatening.

She ventured down to that fence one day and found a man pacing there. She watched for a while and when she thought it was safe she showed herself and let him reveal his character by his reaction. He seemed to be friendly enough and no threat. She took that back to her campfire to think on for the night.

She went back to the fence a second day and the same man was there again; walking alone.

"Hello again," he said without looking directly at her. She could tell that he was trying very hard not to be intimidating. She found it touching because she could have torn him to pieces like a single sheet of paper and she knew it. They shadowed each other for a while and he told her stories of his childhood, the friends he once had and the games and sports they had played.

The next day the man was there again. Ellie had brought him food, a sort of bread she had made from mushrooms and wild garlic. He was amazed when she handed it to him. He tasted it carefully and his eyes widened even further.

"What lovely bread, you are full of surprises. If you would talk I am sure you have wonderful stories to tell."

She did not reply. He waited a little to encourage her but nothing came. Instead he spoke more about the children in the camp. He told of the conditions they lived with but also about who they were. He particularly told her about the 'unaccompanied children', a phrase he obviously hated. These were the children abandoned and alone. The ones whose parents were lost or dead, who had no family to care for them and therefore fell to the care of the group, of the camp. In a desperate place like that, where nobody had enough even for their own most basic needs it was hard for these little ones to get by.

That night Ellie thought about the children. She felt a sadness grow inside her the intensity of which was strange to her. She set to work producing food to busy herself and put those thoughts from her mind.

The following day Dr. Aziz was surprised to find the girl waiting for him inside the fence with a look that meant business set on her small face. For a moment he was frightened of her for what reason he couldn't tell but the feeling passed.

She had little piles of bread and wild plants around her and she spoke one quick sentence as she pointed to them.

"For the children who are alone."

"Come with me," the Doctor replied.

They walked a short distance through the muddy temporary streets of the camp. Thin, weary people raised their heads to look at them but none could hold Ellie's gaze.

They came to a tent erected near some makeshift latrines. The smell was powerful and not pleasant. Dr. Aziz opened the flap and gestured for Ellie to follow.

"These are our little ghosts of conflict. We have to try very hard to stop them disappearing."

"Little ghosts of conflict", the phrase cut straight to Ellie's heart. He might have been describing her.

There were twenty-one unaccompanied children in the camp just then.

The oldest was Ahmed, a boy of fourteen from Libya. He had left his home alone with all the money and good wishes his parents could send with him. He was tall for his age and skinny. He had huge, serious brown eyes and radiated a sense of very hard won maturity.

When he arrived at the camp he brought with him two other Libyan children, a brother and sister, the girl called Mona and the boy named Ibrahim who he had found along the way, shepherding them on the journey with the carefulness of an aging headmaster. They looked to Ahmed now as they would to a parent and they would rarely leave his side.

There were fifteen Syrian children in all. From Farid and Iman, thirteen year old twins, to little Walid who was all of five years old.

There were two girls from Somalia, sisters of seven and six called Calaso and Ikraan and a single Iraqi boy, An. He was eight years of age and quiet, feeling himself more isolated than he truly was because he was the lone child in the tent from his country.

The youngest was a girl of roughly three years old. She barely spoke and seemed not to know her own name. She had been brought to the camp by two women who had picked her up walking alone on the road. The women had broken the fence and made a break two weeks ago. The little girl who had lost her name was still here. Dr. Aziz called her 'Curly' because of her head of thick, black curls but he longed for the day when she might correct him.

The doctor looked after them as well was he could. He found them whatever food was available and did his best to keep them healthy, warm and clean but it was not easy. Conditions were difficult for everyone in the camp and the weakest can get left out when basic resources are scarce.

When Ellie entered the tent, Ahmed, who had good reason to feel himself to be the grown-up of his group, immediately approached her. He saw, and smelled the food she was carrying and it pleased him but he had learned the value of suspicion. He also sensed something dangerous about this girl. He screwed up his courage and made himself as tall as possible.

Ellie's instinct was to give him a hard look, perhaps to slap him down and put him in his place in order to establish her dominance immediately but she didn't.

Instead she found herself placing a hand gently on his shoulder and smiling a small but reassuring smile.

Chapter 25

Wilhelmina held her breath; partly because she was shocked by what she had just watched and partly because she might have a break in her case. It might actually BE a case after all. Best of all, Hungary was not all that far away.

However, before she allowed herself to become too excited, she went back over the details one more time.

It started in Moldova. A familiar story- the murders of some gangsters who were heavily involved in dog fighting. She had the notes from the local police breaking down the number killed and how they died. She had the crime scene photographs and copies of the criminal records of the victims.

Unusually, she had the eye-witness reports of the survivors and even more remarkably she had tape of the crime. Whereas before, any surveillance cameras had always been disabled, in this instance one had been present and working; and allowed to remain that way.

Here was the first piece of hard evidence she had received and it was breath-taking. She watched the footage through one more time.

She watched as a girl, a child really, expertly and ruthlessly killed a number of hardened criminals. It was a strange spectacle; shocking, off-putting but also compelling. The certainty and precision of the child's movements were mesmerizing; the brutality of their consequences terrifying.

The end of the video was especially interesting. Even in the poor quality, grainy footage you could see something happen. A change came over the girl as Wilhelmina watched. Her certainty and decisiveness evaporated and when she fled the crime scene she did so like a frightened child.

From there the girl had been tracked. It had not been easy. She disappeared and reappeared constantly but once they had someone definite to look for it had become possible. Cross referencing with police forces all over Europe a match had been found:

The girl was last seen in a random police photograph of refugees in a camp in Hungary. This was only a week ago and Wilhelmina was going to go there and find her.

Chapter 26

"The Forest of Bad Dreams"; Somewhere in Laos-

The Hyena faced the Crocodile with her head held low, her muscles tight and all the gentleness Ellie had been accustomed to seeing in her eyes burnt away by intense focus and aggression. She growled and spat in her unique fashion and thick saliva ran down from between her giant teeth as they hungered to tear into flesh.

She was ready to kill and a formidable sight to behold. She would have made the blood in most veins run cold with fear but the Crocodile was not frightened and her blood already ran cold. She too was ready to fight. She was hoping for a fight now. The tension between them had built up to the point where only violence would release it adequately and the Crocodile was confident that she could cut the noisy, smelly Hyena down at the knees in moments. Let the Hyena move forward one inch, only one step, and the Crocodile would strike with pleasure.

There had been arguments from the moment they had realised Ellie had gone missing. Arguments about what had gone wrong, what part of her training had been deficient, who had been responsible for that failing, and most heatedly of all, what to do about Ellie now.

All the creatures were involved, all of Ellie's teachers and all the others. Representatives of the entire history of animal evolution and extinction met and argued over what to do about their young soldier now.

The Ape, Crocodile, Wolf, Hare and Hyena had to answer question after question. What might have caused her to break and run? What would she be most likely to do now? Would she talk about what she had experienced? Would anyone believe her? What kind of threat might she pose to them and to their on-going mission?

The Crocodile was amongst the first to state the hardest possible case. She did so simply and clearly-

"She should die. She was always weak. It doesn't matter what has caused her to defy us now and go on the run; some inherent weakness we could not have cured. If she could be any conceivable threat to us we should be rid of her."

"No," the Hare could not stop himself, though he was timid when it came to speaking in the company of his peers, "No, she is one of us. She has lived with us and trained with us. She has given her life to us, worked hard and grown strong. She can be helped, we can bring her back."

"You are fond of her, like a pet," the Crocodile hissed the word 'pet' through her teeth with contempt. "Your foolish feelings are not important now. Action is required. We let them fight when it comes to the test. We see who is strongest then and allow that one will die."

The Hare looked around desperately for support. Shooting imploring looks towards the Ape and the Hyena.

The Ape sat silently and ran his hand across his chin but he said nothing. His golden brown eyes were troubled. He was not yet ready to speak.

The Hyena, on the other hand, had been boiling inside listening to the Crocodile and could hold herself silent no longer.

"What are we, if we break faith with the girl now?"

She paused and stared at each and every animal that could meet her gaze. "Are we not fighting for fairness and justice? Are we not redressing the balance in this world, adding force to the weak to balance the scales of power? We have honour, we have pride, we have loyalty and must keep our word. The test is a fair chance at life as well as death, a fair fight. If we break with that contract than we are fighting for nothing, we become as bad as the humans themselves."

"Words, words, words," the Crocodile mocked, "You have always been too easy with words and too much in love with them. You like ideas and images and you have made a dream of this little human. The facts are the facts and now is the time for action."

"You," the Hyena appealed to the Ape, "You have not yet spoken, "You knew her, you know her, as well as I, she is your ally and your charge, speak for her now."

The Ape emitted a low, troubled, growling noise that seemed to go on for a long time. He was in the midst of a great struggle between his head and his heart. For the first time he was being forced to acknowledge that he loved the little girl like a child of his own and yet that realisation was becoming clear just as he was being forced to accept that she was a danger to them and might well need to be eliminated.

He spoke slowly, taking great care with his words. He was hoping to explain something as much to himself as to his audience.

"I know her, I trained her and I respect her. I know what she can do and what a danger she can be. The human mind is complex and difficult to understand and if she has been pulled back to her own world than she may well become an enemy. If we could capture her and bring her back than maybe…"

"You lack the courage to speak the truth," the Crocodile broke in, "She has turned against us, or at least away from us and there is only one solution, anything else is too great a risk. She must be killed."

The Hyena bristled and dug her claws into the earth in frustration.

And so it went on, first for hours and then for days, until the two most vocal beasts reached the point where neither wanted to speak any more and were ready to fight.

"Enough," the Wolf roared and then strode to the centre of the gathering. "Enough, all of you. This is a sad day.

A sad day for us all." He looked hard at the Crocodile. "Those of us who trained and cared for the girl feel the failure of our mission very deeply." His gaze held down any disagreement from his fellow mentors. "The choice should not be ours, our minds are not clear. A vote must be taken and all should take part except we five. That decision we will accept."

He paused and stood with lowered head, "We will accept."

And so a vote was held. All the representative spirits of the animal kingdom from the beginning of time to the present day took part save only for the ones who had directly controlled Ellie's training and development. They came together to decide whether the girl should die and when they returned their decision the Hyena's wail could be heard all through the forest and far beyond.

Chapter 27

When the noise began Ahmed was on his watch, patrolling the camp and looking for threats. He moved slowly, checking everywhere he could. He took his work seriously.

It was one of the tasks Ellie had given the children and Ahmed, as the oldest and her honorary lieutenant did the most shifts on night duty. He liked the responsibility Ellie had given him. She had recognised his unspoken position as leader of the children and had been careful not to humiliate him.

Since Ellie had arrived in the camp she had taken all of the unaccompanied children under her wing. With Dr. Aziz, she took it on herself to care for them, to make sure they were clean and as well fed as they could be. She had also taken great pains to organise them.

From the biggest to the smallest she assigned them all jobs; they learned to cook for themselves with plants Ellie brought from the outside (Nabil and Rima in particular, were becoming fine and enthusiastic cooks), they boiled their water, they ran through their exercises, they had a time for schooling.

Everything was run to a timetable; everyone had their own responsibilities and all of those responsibilities carried respect. One of those responsibilities was keeping a watch at night.

Dr. Aziz was not entirely comfortable with the somewhat military tone of Ellie's new regime but he had never seen the children so purposeful. They were gaining confidence and definitely getting stronger. The girl was doing something right and he was not going to interfere too much.

Also, he had a sense that it might be dangerous in a manner he could not quite put his finger on to get in her way. Strange, such a good and caring girl but there was an air of menace about her at times that he could not explain.

The noise Ahmed heard this night was like a thunderstorm rolling in from a distance, gathering strength as it came. Ahmed immediately understood that something serious was happening and he went to wake Ellie as he had been trained to do. He discovered her already awake and alert.

He was about to excitedly explain his reason for finding her but she silenced him with a look and motioned for him to follow her. They moved quickly in half crouch by the sides of the tents, making their way towards the source of the noise; an area of the fence on the north side of the camp.

Their eyes widened with what they saw there. There were two large black armoured vehicles breaking through the barrier. They had massive, reinforced front ends and the wire link fence snapped like twigs as they ploughed straight through it. It was like a military assault.

Behind the black tanks Ellie and Ahmed saw a line of single decker buses.

Police in riot gear came through in the wake of the vehicles. Ahmed stiffened and began to stand as if to confront them. Ellie grasped his shoulder and pulled him down. She pointed back to their tent. They ran back there, making no attempt to conceal themselves now.

Ellie wanted to get to the tent before the police. The priority was to keep the children together and keep them safe.

Behind them the police immediately set about dismantling the camp. They pulled people from their shelters and destroyed the canvas structures themselves. When they were finished here, they had been ordered, no one should wish to come back here or have anything to come back to.

They were not brutal but they were rough, using sudden force to take control and shock people out of any idea of resistance. It was shocking to see how quickly and easily this place, which had been home to so many, was being made to disappear.

People were herded into the buses. They moved slowly, but they moved nonetheless and gave no resistance. Many of them were thinking of how they were becoming too used to being herded like this from place to place and how they wished that they could have control over their own lives again, be free to take the basic day-to-day decisions of life that so many take for granted. Others were too exhausted to be thinking much beyond- "I wonder where they are taking me now."

Ellie and Ahmed reached the children in time to help them gather their few belongings. Ellie and the doctor gathered them all together just as the police came and entered the tent.

The young ones were orderly and composed. Dr. Aziz made it understood that they would go quietly where they were directed and that no force would be necessary. The police were taken aback to see the kids lined up like pupils ready to go on a school trip. They were ushered out. One police officer made to place a hand on Qasim's shoulder to move him along but Ellie batted it firmly away. They locked eyes for a second but the officer, not a bully by nature, put his hand down and smiled at the intense girl who did not smile back.

Through the darkness of the night, the violence of the moment and the confusion of their weary minds they were all; the old and young, the weak and strong, the frightened and the numb, driven no more than five miles to a rural railway station.

They were prodded out of the buses and onto a train. It was old, had seen better days and its three coaches were filled with hard, wooden benches.

The doors were closed and locked and a small number of police officers stood guard over the refugees. It was crowded and uncomfortable.

Ellie and Dr. Aziz had made sure that all their group had remained together and been kept safe. They did their best to keep them calm but that was not an easy task. It is asking a great deal of children not to cry or fret when they are taken from their beds in the middle of the night and hauled off to who-knows-where.

The train pulled out of the station slowly. It travelled sluggishly for no more than an hour and then came to a halt under a wide bridge where it stopped again. There it rested as if it were a tired animal and the people inside wondered what would happen to them next.

Chapter 28

Two large, powerful wings beat in the cool night air propelling a bird on its aerial path not far above the tops of the trees. Its face was shaped like a large, slightly, inward-curving dish, pulling the sights and sounds of the countryside into the Ural Owl's mental map of the landscape. She passed like a spectre through the air that gently moved her ghostly black and white feathers and she missed nothing.

Below her on the ground the delicate paws of a Golden Jackal flowed silently and fluently through woods. He moved swiftly like an arrow from the tip of his narrow snout to the end of his remarkably big and bushy tail, until he emerged from the trees onto a back road and turned a sharp corner to approach the rear of an almost abandoned railway station. His eyelids twitched and he shot the gaze of a bright brown eye upwards to see an owl alight on the edge of a bridge directly above an unmoving train; a train so old it might almost have been abandoned there.

The owl emitted a hoarse screech and the jackal answered with his high-pitched howl. Three times they each called and then they fell silent and waited.

Ellie was sitting in the third carriage of the train with one arm around little An. He had finally fallen asleep but his heart rate was still racing with anxiety. She did not envy him his dreams tonight. She heard the cries of the owl and jackal and a chill, a warning signal, ran through her. Perhaps it was nothing, just the normal sounds of the night; but no, she knew deep down, that something, some force was being called up against them. This train was becoming a trap.

On the bridge the owl was joined by another, and then more until the parapet of the bridge was entirely lined on one side by the birds.

Below them the jackal was approached by three of his own kind and then by a number of his much larger relatives. Grey Wolves paced, full of anxious anticipation as more animals arrived. A corps of wild creatures called into action from far off and ready now to do what they had been summoned here for. As they waited they could feel the soil vibrate with the approach of something truly large and powerful.

Ellie heard something landing on the roof of the train- something just a little too heavy. She looked around her. The police officer assigned to guard them was dozing by the door, his breathing was slow and heavy. She slipped her arm from around An slowly and gently, making sure not to wake him. She took one very long, deep breath. She closed and opened her eyes very deliberately once and moved swiftly and silently to a window. She peered through it with some difficulty, as it had not been cleaned in a very, very long time, into the black night.

Initially she could see nothing but as the outside world resolved and pulled into clearer focus she spotted the bright pinpoints of moonlight hitting eyes- the forward facing eyes of predators. They were moving with purpose towards and then around the train, surrounding it. More creatures were alighting on the roof at the same time.

Ellie recognised a trap was about to be sprung and that her best chance to survive and protect the children was to act quickly, to take back the advantage.

She crept up on the police officer, slipped an arm around his neck, pushed a hand into the bend of her elbow and squeezed hard. He needed to be put out of the way with the smallest amount of fuss possible. He would interfere with what she needed to do. He would try to be in charge and besides, she did not have the time to look after him when what she thought was about to happen came to pass.

She took in the people in the seats around her. There were more than just the children she had adopted. It gave her a moment of doubt; but only a moment. She knew where her priority lay.

She woke Ahmed and instructed him in an intense whisper to wake and gather the rest of the children, but quietly, it must be as if they were invisible.

She counted them quickly, all twenty-one were present. She could hear the shallow breathing of the little lungs she was familiar with and then something else, something dissonant, a deeper more powerful breathing reaching her from elsewhere. The hair on the back of her neck stood up in spikes, like the hairs on a hyena's back.

Then the door burst open. It was as if she saw her old mentor the Wolf appearing there out of the night and it froze her for a moment. That moment cost her the initiative and might have cost her much more. The wolf sprang at her and brought her to the ground with too much ease. It opened its jaws wide ready to crush.

Ellie's mind snapped immediately back into the moment. She got to one hip and pushed the wolf's jaws forcefully away from her, tearing her palm as she did so. No time to think about that. She was intent on trying to use the wolf's body to block the narrow entrance to the carriage.

She knew more attackers would be following. She needed to hold them off for as long as possible if the children were to have an opportunity to escape.

A lightening quick glance over her shoulder allowed her to see that Ahmed and the doctor had broken a window and were encouraging the children through it at great speed.

Clever them. And see how brave and disciplined the children were. She was proud of them all. Now she was free to concentrate on the fight.

As she put the wolf down another leapt on her.

She stood her ground in the doorway knowing that as long as she maintained her position there she could not be surrounded and she could reduce the advantage of numbers the animals enjoyed. She must not let the animals get behind her. As the number of jaws and teeth directed against her increased the desire to back up was strong but she fought it as hard as she fought off her attackers, desperate to give the children more time.

Ahmed pushed the last of the children out of the window and then followed. As his feet hit the ground he looked around them and instinctively directed his charges towards some woods he spotted in the near distance.

"Run," he shouted and took off dragging, pulling and encouraging the children. Behind him he could not hear the light tread of two large lynx; compact and muscular cats, who had been watching and waiting for anyone trying to make an escape in that direction but he knew well enough that he must move and keep the children moving. He had not time to notice that Dr. Aziz had not followed.

For Ahmed the short distance to the trees was terrifying and frustrating in equal amounts. The other children could not run as fast as he could and he had to constantly slow down and speed up to keep his charges moving at the fastest possible pace. He was leading like this from the rear when the first lynx sprang on him and brought him down hard to the ground, knocking the air right out of him and leaving him gasping for breath.

Ellie was ready to abandon her position by now. The children were out of the train and on the move. She was waiting for the best moment to break away from the fray and follow them when she saw the bear thundering towards the train like an angry brown mountain of muscle, teeth and claws. The moment to move had suddenly arrived.

She threw herself across the carriage as the bear swung its massive paws, launching wolves out of its way in its eagerness to reach its target. It exploded into the train like a flood breaking through a dam. Ellie felt its breath at her heels as she launched herself headlong through the window and followed Ahmed and the others. The bear began smashing its way through the side of the train in pursuit.

Ahmed could not resist the two lynx that now attacked him. He was too tired and scared and the creatures, though not huge, were so fast and ferocious. His body trashed and beat at the lynx on instinct but his mind had already resigned itself to his fate.

He saw the children reach the edge of the woods and disappear inside and he was happy. Life had been so difficult for so long. He was exhausted and with all his heart and all his might he had done a good job protecting his friends. He loved those children and maybe, just maybe they had a chance now. If they did, he had played no small part in giving it to them. Maybe that was all he was meant to do in this life and maybe that was enough. If that was the test of his worth then he felt he could honestly say he had passed.

Ellie could see Ahmed struggling with the two cats. Although her lungs were already burning she pushed herself even harder to get to him, to help him. Behind her the bear ripped through the side of the train as if it was a can of tinned food and emerged with the force of a hurricane. Its claws tore great chucks of earth up as it sprinted after her. It was completely focused on killing this girl.

More than that, since this urge had possessed it and led it from its home in the Romanian mountains on a journey it would never have taken of its own free will, it was set on destroying her, reducing her to smaller and smaller pieces until it was as if she had never existed. The burning in his head and the pulsing in his muscles would not stop until he had achieved this one essential thing.

Ahmed closed his eyes and tried to think of his parents and his home. He had an instinct that the way he left this life might in some way influence what might happen next. He would have no time to think about that further or deeper.

Ellie channelled strength she didn't know she possessed into the power of her grip. She put her whole self into it and grasped each lynx by the back of the neck and ripped them from Ahmed.

She turned and flung the startled cats at the approaching bear. They impacted the giant in its huge chest and broad face and in their fright and anger bit and clawed at him wildly.

Without looking at what happened next Ellie pulled Ahmed to his feet and half dragged, half carried him after the others.

Sirens blasted in the near distance and the cries of owl and jackal rang out. The bear stood over the ruined bodies of the two lynx and stared into the woods, even more full of murderous rage now. The owls and the jackals called again and again. The bear rose up on its hind legs and roared as if something sharp and barbed were being ripped from its deepest soul but then it turned away from the woods and ran to follow the other animals in retreat.

Chapter 29

That night Ellie lay awake for hours before she finally found sleep. She had driven the children harder than they had ever been driven. She had pushed them, running and walking; crying and silent, until they had put miles between them and the railway station. She had kept them moving, putting one foot in front of the other, falling, being lifted back to their feet; sometimes being carried, sometimes dragged until her own panic had reduced in its intensity enough for her to rest.

Building camp had been hasty and messy. No one was in the right frame of mind to make shelter, build a fire and take watch. They did the best they could. Ellie had pushed the children very far and realised that the small ones were getting dangerously close to their breaking point.

If it had been hard to cover all that ground; it was perhaps harder to be still now and deal with the thoughts that came.

Now she was lying under the most hastily constructed of shelters trying to slow her mind just a little and failing completely.

She was trying to come to terms with the implications of the night's attack. The animal spirits who raised her had clearly cast her aside. She was now the hunted. In her experience that meant one thing- death. Every way she looked at it, it came back to that.

If it had only been herself then she would have been tempted to simply find a place to make a last stand. She knew that she could make herself a very costly target. Whatever came for her would pay a heavy price for her skin. She could spill a lot of blood before they finally brought her down but she had the children to care for now. They needed her.

For the first time that she could remember Ellie had a problem that seemed impossible to solve. No amount of hard work would fix it. She could not simply work harder, train harder, plan more intelligently, build a better strategy. The ones who had taught her the meaning of hard work, the ones who had trained her, the ones who had formed her intelligence and introduced her to strategic thinking were the same ones who now stood against her.

How could she defeat the very ones who had made her? And yet she had no right to lose this battle, too many others now depended on her strength and her cunning.

She was also thinking of the others, particularly the children, the ones with guardians, who had not fallen under her protection; who had been left behind on the train. How many of them were injured or worse now? Had she somehow let them down? How much responsibility did she carry and exactly to whom?

And where was Dr. Aziz? She had become so fond of him. His presence even made her feel more secure somehow, though it was she who protected him in truth. She had not seen him since the train and she feared the worst.

She felt her heart pulled in directions she could not remember it ever having been pulled before, at least not for many years, not while she was living this life.

Ellie was wide awake, looking up at the stars and lost in these thoughts.

At some point eleven year old Yara began to sing. She too had been lying awake, still frightened and confused by the events of the previous twenty-four hours. She was trying really hard to remember her mother. She did this whenever she was really frightened. She tried to clear her mind of anything but these good memories. She tried to recall her mother's smell, the gentle scent of lavender that she had carried with her.

The lyrics of the song were sad ones. They told of an old woman, looking back on her life and mourning her lost youth but it was the sound that Yara loved not the words. Her grandmother had sung this song to her mother and her mother had in turn sung it to her. It reminded her of being tucked up in bed, feeling safe, cosy and loved.

Her voice was small and uncertain to begin with but as she squeezed her eyes tightly shut and the images grew clear and stronger in her mind it became stronger and clearer. It was a good voice, not trained but full of emotion; a voice that was simple and true.

Ellie should have told the girl to be quiet, their camp should be a silent and secret thing but she found herself unable to speak up. She wanted to listen to the girl sing.

Music and songs were a trouble to Ellie. She was surprised and confused by the power they had to stir up emotions in her like rocks thrown into the waters of her mind. She had heard none from the time she had been taken from the Burnhams until she had started going out on missions years later. Then they came to her like spectres; haunting and disturbing her, both familiar and uncanny in equal measure. Tonight she could only listen and let the feelings wash over her.

All the children heard Yara's song and it reached inside them and called up their own memories or dreams of happier, softer times, either in the past or the imagined, hoped for, future. Her song grew stronger, rising up into the night sky, covering them all like a blanket until she became too weary to continue and sleep came late but at last to the camp.

Chapter 30

Wilhelmina Benjamin stood with her mouth agape and her eyes wide. She could not have said with certainty if she shivered because of the cold night air or because of the scene that confronted her and she did not have time to ponder that question now.

It looked like a child had ripped a toy train apart in a fit of anger but it was a real train and there were real casualties, many of them. They were being treated around her; some of them were already beyond treatment.

It had taken forever to get permission to intercept the refugee train. She had intended to do so in a low-key manner and had been unhappy when she had been informed that she would only be allowed to go under the supervision of local police officials- sirens, flashing lights and all. She was very glad that they had come with her now.

The police and medics were here in large numbers and everywhere they were busy with their work. Wilhelmina had been mostly forgotten and was free to move about the site looking for her suspect.

She had quietly searched enough to be certain the girl she was chasing was not here but there were others, some of them able to talk, a few of those willing to do so, who told a compelling story. A story she might not have believed if they had not all basically told the same one and if she had not already felt soaked to the skin in strangeness.

The train had been attacked by wild animals. No one was in any doubt about that. People remembered the wolves and the bear because they were so large, fearsome and yet so unlikely; but they were sure that there were other, smaller animals involved also. Something else, it did seem that there was a particular group of children missing, the ones who were on their own. Yes, the girl in the photograph had been with them. She had looked after them along with the Syrian doctor.

As Wilhelmina moved among the less injured and encouraged them to talk she noticed a familiar figure. A distinguished looking middle-aged man that she recognised. She approached him slowly. She did not want to startle him; she did not want him to run. He seemed to be uninjured, just shaken up and upset.

"Dr. Aziz?" she extended a hand in greeting towards him.

Chapter 31

In the days following the attack on the train Ahmed began to change. It was not the result of any choices he made, or any desire he had to do so. He noticed the things that were happening within him as if he were standing outside himself, watching, almost as if he were a separate person.

The process was out of his control. Too many things had been out of his control and for far too long. It made him tense. It made him anxious.

Before Ellie arrived he had been a quiet, reserved character. The things he had experienced on his journey across Europe had made him suspicious, someone who watched much and spoke only when he had to, when he was sure of the response his words would provoke. He had only asked questions to which he already knew the answers; he only made statements when he was certain of the response they would receive.

After Ellie arrived and informally established him as her second-in-command he had relaxed somewhat. With Ellie around he felt safer than he had for a long time, he felt more purposeful too and he became more like the happier, more out-going boy he had been when was he was younger, when he was still at home with his family. He was older and more experienced certainly and some scars would never heal both physically and mentally but he felt like he was taking back some level of power over his own life. Ellie also released him from some of the responsibility he felt. She was strong and he could trust her. He was proud to be her number two.

After the attack that slowly growing feeling of security was crushed. He found sleep difficult to come by and he became silent and more irritable with the smaller children. Things that he might before have found amusing just annoyed him. The smaller children became wary of the new sharpness of his tongue and cast nervous glances in his direction. This, in turn, made him feel guilty and the guilt further irritated him, making him more likely to snap. He thought about this at night and found it hard to fall asleep.

He looked to Ellie for strength but all was not well there either for Ellie had also changed. All this made him angry and fearful but more than anything else it made him feel sad. When Ellie saved him from the lynx he had already given up. In a way it was as if he had really died then. This thought haunted him and shamed him. He wondered if he had the strength to do what he still had to do. He asked himself, would he give in when he was tested?

Ellie had indeed changed. She had been expecting that her former mentors would pursue her but she had held out a small hope that perhaps they would simply let her go; a deep down wish for some measure of softness in the world. Now that hope had been killed in the most brutal manner possible. She was completely cut adrift and felt more alone than she ever had.

They had tried to kill her. They had tried to kill her and they had killed others; people who were innocent. The people on the train were lost, unhappy, weak, scared, tired but they were not enemies as she had understood. The people she had killed were criminals, torturers, callous abusers of power for profit and cruel pleasure. Her friends, yes they were her friends, on the train, were the opposite.

They were creatures trying to survive and find dignity when all strength, power and advantage was stacked against them. They were the caged animals and they deserved help, they deserved a chance, because they still had a chance, all hope was not lost. Everyone of them counted and the Wolf, the Ape, the Crocodile, the Hyena and even the Hare seemed willing to cut them down without so much as a thought.

Was that what she had fought for? How different was she from the dogs who had chased her down on the day of her final test? Was she simply a creature of violence and an agent of death?

She looked at the children around her, huddled close up to a fire she had built and which Ahmed was tending. She rehearsed all their individual names in her head. She noticed how tired and scared they were and she felt, more than anything, the massive weight of responsibility she now had and feared she would not be up to the job. This was her purpose though; this was the mission that meant she was not that senseless killer but something more.

The task was to keep moving. Keep the children safe and fed yes; but above all else, moving.

The idea of England was fixed in her mind. That was her own destination; that was where most of the refugees talked of wanting to go. She would get all these children there with her and nothing; either human or any other kind of animal, would stop her.

From this point on they would move Ellie's way; they would move like animals. They travelled mostly by night and kept consistently off the roads and out of sight of people. They became tight and disciplined in their routine like a military unit.

They woke not long before noon. Three children went to gather food. Ellie went with them initially, until all of them had a good idea of how to find nutritious things. Three others patrolled the camp to make sure they were still secret and secure. Then a fire was started to make the first meal of the day.

They prepared the food and sat together talking. Afterwards Ellie ran them all, even the smallest of them, through a series of exercises.

After a rest Ellie organised them into classes and helped them with what she saw as the basics of education.

Later they ate again, a larger meal.

They broke camp as the sun set and walked through most of the night. When they had done their miles Ellie choose another safe place to camp, teaching them all how to find such a place, and they prepared a fire. If it was cold they lit it, if not it remained unlit until the morning.

As the days passed the children settled into their routine and began to enjoy it. They got stronger and felt more capable. They were better fed, cleaner and more engaged than they had ever been in the camps.

They crossed from Hungary into Austria. They tried not only to stay away from towns and cities, but also farmland. They followed trails through the mountains and the places they travelled through were beautiful. After so long being starved of beauty it gladdened their hearts. The air was fresh and the water they drank from the mountain streams was clean, clear and refreshing.

They did not know exactly when they crossed over from Austria to Switzerland and they cared as little as did the mountains themselves.

Sometimes they came into contact with farmers tending to their cattle in the high pasture but they always spotted them first because they were moving with organisation. Ahmed and some to the older children took the lead, the smallest children were safe in the middle, and Ellie took up the rear, watching all. She was proud of her little band and that pride allowed her to sometimes forget her worries and responsibilities. Those were good moments; travelling with her team as if only for the pleasure of it.

There were times, when she heard noises too close to camp at night, when a bird seemed to follow them for too long, when Ellie was brought abruptly back to her tension and anxiety but a certain level of health and happiness was starting to surround this little group, a happier time for all of them. Ahmed began to smile again.

There were nights, clear nights when the sky was an awe-inspiring dome of numberless stars, when all of them felt that they could, and perhaps would, live like this forever. They knew it was not possible, they knew that they were heading back to civilization and to plenty of troubles before too long. They were deliberately going towards all that; but some nights, some sweet nights they allowed themselves to fall asleep believing that they had found a new way to live and would live this way for the rest of their lives.

When they crossed into France it was time to turn
north. At first the mountainous landscape remained
unchanged but as they put down the miles they were forced
onto lower and lower ground.

They had to be more careful now. It was harder to
remain concealed but they continued. They were all
possessed by their mission and by a growing belief that
they just might succeed.

Chapter 32

Officer Benjamin and Dr. Aziz-

The room was extremely small. There was just enough room for the table and two chairs. It smelled of stale coffee and cigarette smoke and, of course, it had no windows. It was like sitting and waiting inside a sealed, grey tin box. Dr. Aziz imagined he might find himself sealed up in there and forgotten.

The seat he had been directed to occupy was appropriately hard and uncomfortable. No matter how he moved about he could not find himself an easy position.

Still he was out of the cold night air and away from that dreadful train. He was warming up a little and calming down slowly.

He had been reluctant to leave the train and the people he was attending to until he had seen that medical staff were caring skilfully for the wounded. Once he had seen the paramedics doing their work, however, his strength had failed and he had deflated as some of the tension started to leave him. He had put up only a little protest as two police officers lead him away.

They had brought him a short distance to a run-down looking municipal building in a small country town and deposited him in this room before leaving without a word.

They had not even bothered to lock the door. If they assumed that he was too exhausted and shocked to make a break for freedom they were absolutely correct.

There was no clock on the wall and he had no watch or mobile phone so he had no accurate idea of how long he was sitting there alone before the door opened again.

The look and demeanour of the person who entered the room was a surprise. He could not define exactly why but she seemed out of place. Perhaps it was simply the fact that she appeared kind. Anyone even a little human would be out of place in this room.

She was a tall woman, somewhere in her mid-thirties he would guess. She wore a practical, grey suit that looked like it was usually kept well cleaned and pressed but had been over-worn in the previous days and could do with some ironing now.

The woman wearing the suit looked somewhat worn also, tired from days without proper sleep.

She had a determined set to her face and looked strong but under the circumstances what Dr. Aziz noticed most was the compassion he thought he could detect in her eyes.

"Hello," she spoke native English with an accent the doctor could not place. "My name is Wilhelmina Benjamin. I work for Interpol. I understand that you have had a very difficult time but I have some questions to ask you and I would very much appreciate it if you could give your answers some thought and give me as much information as you can."

Doctor Aziz said nothing but his nod was not unfriendly and he waited for her to continue.

Wilhelmina looked at the man across the table from her. He looked exhausted; his eyes were blood shot and his skin had an unhealthy, grey tone. It was hard to get a good idea of his age. Hard times always made people look older than their years.

He had already told the police that he was a Syrian and a Doctor. Ragged and overused as he appeared to be; he nonetheless had the air of a person who was done with playing games. Wilhelmina decided to put her cards on the table. She felt that this was a man who would respond best to the direct approach.

"Dr. Aziz, I am looking for a particular girl."

She paused to let that statement sink in and to read his reaction. He gave little away.

"I have no interest in immigration issues," Wilhelmina continued, "That is not part of my investigation or my job. I am investigating a series of serious and violent crimes. The girl I am looking for has, I think, a connection to these crimes. I believe you know this girl. I have at least one photograph of you with her. I think that you may well have a positive relationship with this girl and you may wish to protect her. I am not interested in harming her but I need to find her and to find out what is going on with her and if she is connected to the criminal matters of which I speak."

She placed a photograph on the table, turned it to face him and pushed it towards him gently with her index finger.

Dr. Aziz looked at the photograph. It was a poorly focused image, probably the type of thing that the police would occasionally take when they patrolled the outside of the fence at the camp. It clearly enough showed the Doctor himself and the strange girl who had arrived at the camp and become the guardian of the most vulnerable children- his friend. In fact it showed her directing him to go get some water like a strict teacher instructing a pupil.

He was unsure what he should do next. Should he tell this officer what she wanted to know? Did he trust her? Did she really have the interests of the girl at heart, even a small amount? Of course he could not be sure. Maybe he could try to tip the balance in favour of the girl somewhat.

"If you would like me to help you find her, you will have to take me with you."

"Excuse me Doctor but..., you do know how serious this is don't you? This girl is possibly involved in violent crimes."

"I understand that you are investigating that possibility," the Doctor spoke slowly and carefully, "But let us say I have a connection with this girl and I can be of some help to you in finding her, then I might be of great assistance to you in talking to her and dealing with her should you actually find her. IF I am with you when that happens. If.."

He let the idea hang in the air between them. He had said his piece. It was up to her now.

Wilhelmina thought. She thought hard. She rubbed her tired eyes and thought some more.

Dr. Aziz added-

"I am resigned to staying here if I have to but I would like to go with you. I would like to do what I can to help the girl you are after. Whatever you know or think you know about her, she has shown herself, as far as I have seen, a strong and admirable person."

Now he was finished.

Wilhelmina sighed.

"It won't be easy. It won't be easy to get you out of here and if I do then you will be in my custody. Whatever the legal situation, you will be in my custody. You will do what I tell you to do at all times. You will be there to help me to do my job and if you interfere with that in any way…"

She let the threat colour the tone of her voice.

Dr. Aziz nodded, just once.

"And you will talk to me. You will tell me what you know."

After a short delay he nodded again.

"I will try, but if I can't get you out of here you will still tell me everything you can. I know you don't know me but please understand I am trying to do the right thing. For the girl, for... well, the right thing all round."

The pause was longer than before. Dr. Aziz was well practiced at keeping his emotions out of his face but it was clear to see that he was torn. After more than a minute of silence, close to the point where Wilhelmina would have stood up and left, he nodded slowly.

"Ok then," she said, slapping her hand on the table, "Wait here, I think I have a lot of persuading to do."

Chapter 33

The Children:

They trooped into the port town of Calais by night. All of them were feeling nervous; their senses on high alert. Calais is a large town, they had watched its lights growing closer for a long time as they approached, and as such it was full of danger for them but it also faced the south coast of England across the narrowest part of the English Channel and so it was to be the last stop before they finished their long, arduous journey.

Ellie led them to an industrial area at the edge of the town and there they stopped. There were no houses here and most workers had gone home for the night by the time the children slipped in quietly. They kept themselves hidden from the few homeless people they saw getting ready to sleep on the streets of the area.

Calais had recently become intimately connected with the issue of refugees. Many, hoping to reach Britain, had gathered in a number of camps not far from the centre of the town. The largest, which had been dubbed "The Jungle", had become notorious for its size and its squalor. More than six thousand souls were living there without the basic facilities that make life in such numbers sustainable and bearable. They had no proper way to stay clean or fed. They did not have the opportunity to look to their children's education. They did not have access to medical care. They had few rights and protections under the law. Some had hidden or thrown away their passports so that they could not be identified and returned to their countries of origin and therefore they were stateless and even nameless.

There would be no more camps for Ellie and her charges. They would not put themselves behind any more fences or barriers. There was no question of that.

Ellie's job was to get them a boat and get them moving on with the minimum delay. She intended to spend the absolute least amount of time she could in Calais.

This ran Ellie head on into a difficult problem; a new problem for her. For as long as could remember she and felt justified in taking what she needed on a mission by any means necessary. She had never wanted to hurt anyone not directly targeted by her mentors but she had felt that she was allowed to bully, to intimidate, if the circumstances made it necessary.

Now that reasoning was gone. She had to think far more about what she did and how she went about it. She would protect the children at all costs but she had to respect the lives and rights, even the property, of others also. Property had meant nothing to her before but now she had a growing awareness of how fundamental some possessions could be for people. Life was suddenly a lot more complex.

Still, she was going to get the children through this bottleneck without delay, the whole place smelled like a trap to her.

She went to the beach. She walked along the sand and took mental note of the vessels she found there. There were small sailboats, pleasure boats and fishing boats. Her eyes came to rest on a large dingy with a powerful outboard motor. This boat would take them across the twenty or so miles to England quickly and safely.

She made her way nearer to it, pretending only the most casual interest. There was a chain on the motor. It was a heavy, impressive-looking chain with a large padlock. She knew at least five ways to break them open and if no one was around to oppose her she would do the job that night but first she needed to acquire a tool.

It took her less than an hour to find a boat shed with its door slightly ajar. She slipped in and searched until she found what she needed. A strong iron crowbar. Then she was gone, waiting for the sun to set.

Chapter 34

Wilhelmina and Dr. Aziz:

They drove in silence and through the darkness for over an hour. Both of them had things they wanted to say and yet each, for their own reasons, needed a period of silence more.

Dr. Aziz sat with his eyes closed trying to resist the pounding headache that seemed determined to split his skull and Wilhelmina drove peering with great concentration out the window of the small car and through the rain that beat just as heavily as the doctor's headache on the outside of the windscreen.

"You know I hate driving in the rain. It makes me nervous and driving in a foreign country..."

Wilhelmina had broken the silence without having consciously decided to. She really did hate driving in the rain. Strange, no matter how serious the situation, little things like that never changed.

Dr. Aziz opened his eyes and stopped rubbing his temples. He looked through the car window.

"This is not a pleasant night for driving that's for sure." He agreed.

They fell back into silence. This time as they travelled on the silence built tension until Dr. Aziz spoke again.

"The girl has a good heart. You should know that."

He had brought up the subject that concerned them both; the reason they were together in this car.

"That may well be true Doctor but she may also be very dangerous."

There it was, in two sentences they had laid out the whole problem. It seemed that they had seen two sides of the same person and were both struggling to understand what the existence of the other side might mean.

"What is it you think she has done?"

"I think that she may have killed people, maybe a lot of people."

Dr. Aziz found that hard to believe; but somehow, not as hard as he would have liked. For a few moments he was not sure what to say. In the end and mostly on instinct, he changed the subject slightly.

"She was a native English speaker. I am sure of that."

Wilhelmina was not altogether unhappy herself that the conversation had altered course.

"And her name?"

"I did not learn her name. She did not speak much about herself. She did not speak much at all."

"And yet you are sure..."

"Sure that she is an native English speaker, yes."

"And did she say where she was going?"

"No, but she was on a well trodden path. We all were. I think she will go to France and from there she will try to cross the channel to England."

"Hmm, well, I have sent her photograph to the police in both France and England. Who knows, she may be picked up along the way. It may even be possible to identify her. I mean find out her name and where is comes from. She certainly is a mystery at the moment."

"So, we are going to Calais then?"

"It certainly looks that way."

Chapter 35

Calais; France:

It was difficult to coax the children into the boat. Most of them were understandably terrified of the sea, having experienced dreadful crossings from their homelands to Europe. Ellie did her best to be patient. She knew that they would find the courage. They always did. It was one of the things she loved about them, this seemingly endless well of bravery in the face of so many obstacles. Soon, she hoped, they would all have a chance to rest from all this testing of their bravery but not yet.

They could not have wished for better conditions. It was a clear night. The channel was calm. With luck the journey would be swift. That was good- Ellie had no desire to spend a second longer on the water than she had to.

As they drifted away from the shore all twenty-two people on board were silent. Each of them was holding their breath, some of them with eyes closed tight, wishing the minutes and seconds away until they reached the relative safety of dry land again.

The engine was the only sound. In the first minutes it was almost too loud. Ellie wished it could be quieter; but then she forced herself to associate the noise with speed, with a swift journey, and the idea gave her heart.

Ellie constantly scanned the water for danger. The route was busy. There were cargo ships and ferries at all times here but she was looking for the Coast Guard or Police, anyone who might interfere with them. Perhaps someone on one of the passing vessels might report them to the authorities but she was banking on the speed of their dingy getting them to England before they could be captured.

They made good progress. The night was pleasant. The sky was like many that had comforted Ellie during hours spent under the stars.

They were more than half way across.

Some of the children seemed to be relaxing a little but Ellie kept eyes just as alertly focused on the way ahead. She might have done better looking for signs of movement just below the water's dark surface.

Not far beneath the water, travelling at great speed, was one of the most perfect predators nature has ever produced. A unique monster of teeth and muscle, born in the Mediterranean Sea, no member of its species had ever travelled quite this far north before. Its greatest instinct was to hunt and to kill and it was that instinct that was being directed towards the English Channel and one particular fast moving vessel that night.

Millions of years of evolution had pointed this great beast towards this end on this night and nothing living could be more directed or more determined. It was thirty feet of grey death honed since before humans appeared on the Earth.

A fin broke through the water. The shark was close but Ellie had not seen it. It was Fatima who saw it. Her eyes opened wide and her hand sprang to her mouth. In that first moment she could hardly believe what she was seeing but something in her gut told her she was not deceived. She pointed out to the back of the boat and screamed:

"Look, look there!"

Ellie turned to look but saw nothing. The fin had disappeared below again.

"What is it?" she asked Fatima, trying to keep the fear from her own voice. But Fatima could not catch her breath. She struggled to get command of herself. Ellie directed Ahmed to take control of the motor and moved in beside the frightened girl.

"It was there..." she struggled with her broken English as she pointed insistently. "There, out there!"

They were still moving forward, all the time getting closer to the coast of England. They could see it now, their hoped for destination, getting nearer. Everyone on the dingy hoped, willed, prayed for this journey to be over.

Ellie squeezed Fatima's hand and whispered to her to be strong. She asked Ahmed to remain at the motor and she went to the back of the boat scanning all around for any sign of danger.

Perhaps Fatima was mistaken but the way she shook told a different story. They were nearly there, just a little more time, all they needed was a little more time. They deserved it. Surely they would get it. Then something big hit the dingy from below.

The vessel left the water and was lifted several feet into the air. It came crashing down again throwing its occupants around like rag dolls.

Then everyone saw the fin, out in front of the boat now. Ellie made a quick count, all the children were still in the boat, clinging onto whatever they could for all they were worth.

The fin came forward relentlessly and then a giant head rose out of the water and opened wide its death-dealing mouth with its rows and rows of jagged, spear head teeth. It clamped down on the front of the boat and began to shake.

Ellie grabbed the crowbar and leapt forward. She beat down on the Great White's nose with all she had. She rained down blows for nearly a minute before the beast let go and sank below again.

Were the children all there? Yes, yes they were. The shark circled off to the left and began another attack. Ahmed turned the dingy sharply to try to outrun the monster, at least to buy some time.

Ellie had seconds to make a decision. The shark was closing in to attack again. The boat would be destroyed or overturned. A picture of the children thrown into the water, left in the sea with this great killing machine flashed into her mind and a moment later she acted.

She clung onto the crowbar with white-knuckle tightness and sprang into the water, swimming directly towards the shark.

Chapter 36

Harriet and Marcus:

They sat side by side on a long, cold bench in a grey, featureless corridor in a grey, featureless building. There was something about being made to sit like this, in a place like this that made them feel powerless, like school children waiting for punishment from the head teacher or criminals awaiting sentence. The repressive atmosphere made them irrationally afraid to speak; as if somewhere near them, someone important was holding a stern finger to their lips.

They had not known how close together to sit. Unconsciously they had taken positions so close they were almost touching. That somehow felt too intimate for their present relationship and they silently shuffled back and froth without even knowing they were performing this awkward dance until they had created a safer distance between then.

There was a single lonely window in the corridor, set too high up in the wall for them to see anything but the grey afternoon sky through it. Outside, of course, it was raining.

When they had been contacted and asked to come to this ugly and depressing police public relations building they had immediately known it must be about Ellie and a great mass of confused and overpowering emotions had crashed in on both of them with overwhelming force.

The people who contacted them would give them no details. They were polite and apologetic and stressed that the appointment had been made as soon as possible so that Marcus and Harriet would not have to suffer in ignorance for any longer than absolutely necessary but no information could be given out over the phone and, besides, no definite or concrete information was available. That was all that could be said.

Harriet had called Marcus a few moments before he had been able to call her.

"Did they call you?" she asked, "Did they tell you anything?"

Both their voices trembled with emotion as they spoke. They had decided to say nothing to Tristan yet, not until they knew more. Then they had simply had to wait, the feeling that a huge hand was crushing their chests constantly present.

A day and a half later, waiting outside the door of a Mr. Penrose's office both Ellie's parents were still shaking. Neither had taken a full breath for thirty-six hours. Marcus rested a hand between them on the bench and Harriet placed a kind hand of her own on his and smiled at him. He nodded in return. They would always be connected, deep down.

The door opened and Mr. Penrose; a large, jolly-looking man who appeared to require some effort to sustain a grave look and stop the loose flesh of his face dancing, ushered them into his office and asked them to sit. There were two other people in the room. Mr. Penrose introduced them:

"This is Officer Benjamin," he indicated a tall, athletic looking woman who looked like she needed a good night's sleep, "She is with Interpol and the gentleman there is Dr. Aziz, he is," here there was a pause while he casually pointed at a distinguished but equally tired looking man in his fifties and tried to form the correct phrasing, "…He is assisting Officer Benjamin at present."

"Hello," Wilhelmina began, and Mr. Arthur Penrose was very pleased that she was taking over, "Thank you both so very much for coming in. (As she was saying the words Wilhelmina already felt stupid. Of course they would 'come in' when they had been essentially told they would receive some important information about their missing child.) I am sorry that you have been kept in suspense and so I will get quickly to the point of my being here. There is a possibility that we may be able to help each other. Before I say anything else I would like you to look at a photograph please. Then everything will be clearer for all of us."

Wilhelmina handed Harriet a large, black and white photo print. She held it so that her former husband could also see.

The moment before their eyes focused on the correct part of the image felt like an eternity. It was a picture taken through a fence. It was somewhat grainy, not the best quality. The backdrop was squalid; tents in a sea of mud but there near the centre was a young girl.

They took hold of each other's hands once again on instinct and squeezed hard. Tears instantly came to their eyes. It was difficult to speak. Then Harriet managed-

"Oh God.." and she pointed at the photograph, "It's her, it's Ellie.."

Marcus could only nod his assent.

With the greatest effort Harriet composed herself-

"Where was this taken; when was this taken? Where is she?"

Mr. Penrose answered-

"We are not altogether sure as of right now.."

"The photograph was taken in Hungary," Wilhelmina interrupted, "it was taken by a police officer at a refugee camp within the last month. I'm sorry to say we got to the camp too late to find her but we think that she may well already be travelling to England."

"Just a moment," Marcus had found this voice, "this is a lot to take in but who are you? We haven't met you before I'm sure. What is your role here? Where is our daughter now?"

Wilhelmina took a deep breath. She had been dreading this, trying not to think about it. Now she was closing in on the moment when she must confront these poor people with the joyful fact that their little girl was still alive and then instantly add the possibility that their dear child was some sort of vicious criminal, a dangerous wild animal or some combination of the two.

Dr. Aziz was lost in his own thoughts- "So, I know her name now. Eleanor Burnham, Ellie. The name comes with a whole history attached. Look, a family, a place in the world, in the social order of this country. This name is a single link in a chain of history. And yet it is an interrupted history. Does this name still have meaning for this girl, the girl I know from the camp? How will she reclaim that name and all that goes with it? Can she do so? Will she be allowed to?"

He had met far too many children with interrupted histories, far too many young lives uprooted from the strong sustaining soil of their own stories. How difficult would it be for them to build new stories, stories that could include their pasts, present and futures? How easy would it be for their stories to become twisted and unhealthy?

Meanwhile, Wilhelmina was speaking slowly and carefully. She was doing her best to lay out the story she had to tell as honestly as she could. It was clear that the parents had not been contacted by the girl. They obviously knew nothing of the girl's whereabouts or her activities since her disappearance. She tried to balance the needs of this family with the reality of her own investigation. There was no good way to do it but she hoped she might find one of the least bad ways.

"We will be circulating this image. We will be doing absolutely everything we can to find your daughter. We would like your help; if she contacts you for instance we would like you to inform us. We want to return your daughter safely to you but we also have a context to work in here. We need to understand her possible role in certain very serious incidents. Much is not clear in this story but we need to understand it."

She explained how Dr. Aziz became a part of the story. Marcus and Harriet stared at him with jealous, hungry eyes. This man had known their daughter as she was now better than they did. They had many, many questions for him and he was keen to answer them as best he could.

They sat and talked for a long, long time. Long past the time when Mr. Penrose should have been sitting in his train home.

*Chapter 37*

Ahmed:

Ahmed ran the terminally damaged dingy headlong onto the shingle beach. For a full thirty seconds he sat with his left hand grasping the tiller, his gaze fixed intensely ahead.

Then, slowly, Calaso and Ikraan came to him and lifted his hand gently. They led him off the boat and all the other children followed.

They huddled together on the beach. Each one was checking that all the others were there. Each one was feeling the same mix of emotions.

They had made it. They had travelled from places that had been written off. They had passed through countries, whole countries, that did not want to know them, that saw them as nothing more than a nuisance, they had starved and frozen, they had walked beyond the capabilities of their children's bodies and they were here.

Each child remembered their own journey. Whether they had fled poverty and hunger, repression or war; whether they had left behind family or the place where their family was buried, each one had fought their way along their own road; each one had had their courage tested over and over and every one had known moments when that courage had failed but they had persisted and had not been broken, at least never completely. They had made their journeys alone and together.

They had arrived. What would happen now, they could not know but they understood that they had done it.

They sat in silence, soaked to the skin. Some of them hugging. They sat and watched the sea and wondered if the girl; the strange, tough girl who had been their friend and protector, would emerge. They sat and they waited.

Chapter 38

At the start of this story I asked you to imagine yourself for a short time inhabiting the body of a dog-that was good practice for a more difficult task of imagination. Now I will ask you to imagine you have the wings and the senses of a bird. Close your eyes and take to the air. Feel the wind lifting you high above the ground and into a clear sky. Beat your wings, feel their strength and your confidence grow; and build up speed.

You are flying over the sea. Look down and see the colours change through a hundred shades of blue and green. Notice the surface of the water constantly changing shape, moving like wind blown sand.

See the cliffs as you arrive in Dorset on the south coast of England. Fields, stone walls, cattle and farm buildings speed by beneath you. You see it all.

Push on and push on further inland. The first town passes below you. Follow the road that leaves the town as it broadens and travels deeper into the countryside.

After only a few more minutes you cross a small river and discover the village of Tolbundle Bridge. Circle the church that sits in the centre of a little graveyard once or twice and glance to your left.

There is a big house there. It has a large front garden with a rusty and disused trampoline.

Behind the house the ground slopes upwards to form a little hill. A figure is standing there with gaze fixed intently on the back door. It is a young girl. She is dirty and her clothes are torn. On the sleeve of her top there is the brownish, red stain of dried blood.

When she closes her eyes she still sees the mouth of the shark… and the large grey eye into which she plunged the crowbar like a spear. She will always live with that image close to her, fear has burned it into her memory forever.

Circle around; once, twice, a third time, above the girl and peer down at her face. Can you read the emotions that are visible there? Fear, uncertainty, determination, a hint of hope?

Yes I think you can detect a hint of hope as she moves towards the back of the house.

A note to the reader:

Firstly, this is a work of fiction. I hope it inspires your imagination to run wild but it is not meant to encourage you to do anything dangerous. I do hope it supports you in exploring your own vast capabilities in terms of your physical performance, imagination (that word again because it is so important) and compassion.

I absolutely endorse a little adventure but please don't go fighting any sharks- they are quite beautiful creatures really.

Secondly, and very importantly, thank you; and keep reading. The adventure will continue...

If you would like to keep up with what is going on in Ellie's world you can go to: 'Animals- the book' on Facebook: https://www.facebook.com/Animals-the-book-2034854743217872

About the author:

Jamie Lynch was born in Dublin, Ireland in the early 1970s. He spent much of his childhood roaming the city centre looking for unusual and exciting places he might one day live in rent-free.

Since then he has had a lot of jobs, travelled a fair amount and read a lot of books. It was in those books he found the place he was looking for as a child.

He now lives in Dorset, England.

Cover Design by: Jason Applin

Printed in Poland
by Amazon Fulfillment
Poland Sp. z o.o., Wrocław

55446843R00179